De

This publication is fiction. Any names associated with real people have had permissions expressly granted to the author and publisher to use their names in this book.

For permissions, write:
Blue Room Books
Attn: Death in E minor 9[mm]
2425 Lawrenceville Highway, #C7, Decatur, GA 30033

Cover design and interior layout:
Angela K. Durden
Editor: Tom Whitfield

DEATH in Eminor 9[mm]
BLUEROOMBOOKS.COM
DECATUR, GEORGIA

DEATH
in E minor 9
[mm]
DURDEN
KELL
Author of "Whitfield, Nebraska"

Prologue

"I owe you no explanation," she said, eyes wide in a man-stimulating pique.

"B-b-but of course you do," he stammered angrily.

She stared at him, then shrugged and shook her head. "D-d-dear boy, you have so much to learn about women." She reached out a fingertip to tap the tip of his nose. He jerked back before she could touch it. "You see? That's why you will never get me in a bed while you are in it." She laughed.

His eyes went dark. He showed teeth in what some might have mistaken for a smile, then growled. "You have no manners. If I took the t-t-time to ask you a question, you should take the t-t-time to answer it. G-g-good manners. See how that works?"

They heard her name called. Their heads jerked toward the stage where Joe beckoned her. "You want to come up and sing us a song?"

She threw a hand up in the air and said, "Hell yeah."

Joe said, "Then come on up, darlin'. Whatcha wanna sing?"

She hollered, "What song do ya want me to sing?"

Joe grinned and said, "How about *Gallows' End* in C. Swing it?"

"Sure, baby. Love it," she said, and walked toward the stage, eyes following her. Some who knew her called her name. She blew them kisses as she swished her backside through the tightly packed tables.

He watched it all with a contempt fueled by envy. "B-b-bitch. She'll be sorry," he mumbled under his breath, then walked out the door just as the Jazz band got down with the opening riffs and she stepped to the mic. He looked through the window and stared at everyone on the stage.

"They'll all be s-s-sorry."

1 Adman Goes To Red Light Café

"Yo, Adman. Where's your case, man? Playing tonight?"

"Maybe. We'll see." I laid a twenty on Mitchie, the door guy.

He palmed it. Slick as a whistle it went into his wad of cash and just as slick out came a ten and a five in change. "Later, man. Good to see ya."

"Back atcha, Mitchie." I stepped past him, opened the door, and walked in the Red Light Café. I turned my head to the left. Ah, the house band was still playing. Turned my head right and saw all the young lions — college students — lined up ready to be called. It was going to be a horn-heavy night. Predominant were saxes, which meant a lot of loud notes and a lot of immature emotion. Jesus.

Listening to some of them play made me feel sorry for the women they dated. If they had sex like they played, then it was nothing but wham-bam-thank-you-ma'am and wasn't-that-grand? Not that any of these guys were having sex. Hell, you could look at them and see that. When the Jazz Kittens walked by you could see their horns stand at attention, but their eyes were like deer caught in headlights.

But who was I to complain too much? Wasn't I the same when I was that age? So focused on my instrument and my talent and style that women were not a reality. I shook my head and smiled. Hell, was it only twenty years ago I lost my cherry? As I passed them, lined up against the wall, I heard "Hey, Adman." Everybody had a fist to bump and were grateful for the smile The Great Adman bestowed upon them.

Yeah, I was their hero. Everything they wanted to be when they grew up. When did I stop feeling like a hero? When did I get tired of adulation? I made my way to the bar in the back where the owner had my usual sitting at an empty spot.

"Start a tab tonight, Adman?"

"Yeah, Michael. Why not." I took a sip of my usual, Jack Daniel's Black American over ice, feeling the warmth travel down my throat and into my gut. I closed my eyes and let myself have a pleasant private thought about my woman. Yeah, that made me smile, but the thought was interrupted.

"Hey, wanna buy me a drink?"

Though I knew the voice and didn't have to look to identify the person, I turned my head to Marilyn. "Sorry. Can't. You're still underage."

She patted my arm. "Just as sweet."

"Come here, woman. Give me a hug."

Marilyn gave me a big hug, squeezing me as tight as she could. I did not squeeze as much. She was eighty. I went easy on her old bones. "What's with the cane?" I got up to give her my stool.

"No, no. I can't climb up there anymore, much less sit for long on them high deathtraps," said Marilyn. "I fell. It was stupid. Thought I broke a hip. But," she waved at it with her free hand, "as you can see, not broke, just bruised. Thank God."

"Yes. Thank God. Hey, you gonna sing tonight? I'll carry you up on the stage. Make a whole production of it. Give 'em some laughs. You can play the chanteuse."

"Yeah. Like the old days. When Jazz wasn't so serious and you didn't need a damn degree to understand it," she said. Small tears threatened to escape.

I hated it when the melancholy came upon her, but that was always the best time for her to sing. I thought I'd cheer her up. "Say, why don't you sing *Can't Seem To Cry Over You*? I'll play Sweet Stella with ya. We'll show the young lions how to do it right, okay? Yeah? Whaddaya say?" I gave her my biggest encouraging smile.

"Eh. Mebbe. I'll see how I feel later."

"Sure." But she was walking away.

Over my shoulder I heard, "*Bednyy dorogoy.*" I looked at Misha. He translated, "Poor dear."

I nodded. Poor dear, indeed. Not too many years from now that will be me and Misha toddling up to the stage. Me, blowing with all I could muster, but not for very long. Misha, alternately pounding and caressing the keys, but his feet not bouncing in time. Folks in the audience clapping for our past glory days and whispers of "Do you know who they used to play with?" circling the room.

My full name is John Cold Dann. I do not know what my parents were thinking when they chose my middle name, I just know that every time I asked about it when I was a kid, they'd look at each other. Dad would grin and Mom would giggle. Then Dad would say, "Son, one day, when yer old enough, we'll tell out." But by the time I was old enough I wasn't about to ask because I had a feeling I didn't want to know Mom and Dad did *that* and knew, somehow, the answer was about *that.*

I was born and raised in the Great State of Georgia, on the far outreaches of Metro Atlanta in a small town called Sharpsburg. Mom and Dad and my siblings still live there. It's just south of

Fayetteville, which is now home to some big-ass film studios.

I now live in Decatur, a city just north and east of Atlanta. You may recall Atlanta was burned down twice. Once in 1864 during the Civil War — or the War Between the States or the War of Northern Aggression, take your pick — and once fifty three years later in 1917 when a fire in the West End got out of control and burned it all down again.

In other words, we native Georgians know how to take a fire and turn it into an opportunity for a good ol' barbeque.

My opinions on music are strong. After all, I am what some call an *artiste*. And, yeah, I'm well known, some even say famous, though I can still walk down the street and not get mobbed. But I make a living with my music one way or another.

Tin Pan Alley, Beale Street, Sixteenth Avenue, and Hollywood and Vine may get more press and have been more commercial, but Georgia is where musical pioneering began. Ray Charles' first big hit was recorded by Bill Lowery at Georgia Tech's radio station WGST. From Ma Rainey to Sonny Terry to the Allman Brothers to James Brown and so many more, the world has heard — and fell in love to — Georgia singing.

Georgians have always done things our way. We might get made fun of. But damn, we are good. And I felt privileged to be involved in bringing Jazz to the forefront and building on the legacy of those who helped define the art form.

Now you know who I am.

I stared at the stage a moment longer, then turned back to the bar and took another slow sip. This time the warmth slid into me, heart and soul.

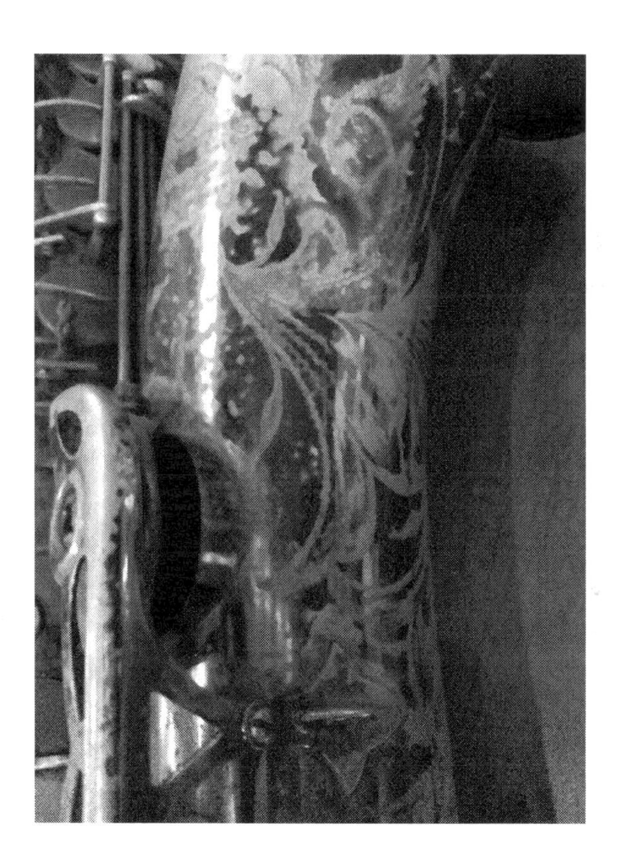

2 Requiem for a Jazz Kitten

The sun was too bright for seven. Normally I would not be awake at this time of the morning, but my phone was blowing up with text tones. I wondered which car warranty had expired, or was it a credit card that was in dire need of being protected? I rolled over with a pillow pulled tight to my head. That did not help much with cutting the sound.

You might be thinking I had a hangover and that's why the tones sounded so loud. You would be wrong. I stopped with the hangovers six years ago. They weren't fun anymore and the bragging rights just weren't worth it, either. I wanted to remember what I had done, what I had played, who I had talked to, and who I had taken home.

Clear memory is the best muse for my artistry.

Throwing covers off, I pushed myself up from the bed. Stood for a couple of moments, stretching, then told my feet to walk. I touched the screen of my iPhone and scrolled through all the on-screen notifications. Thirty texts and not one was about my car warranty or credit score.

I opened Messenger and read through the texts. Oh, man. Harley Rose, stage name of a Jazz Kitten — that's a female singer — had died last night. In her bed. In somebody else's bed. Oh, wait. Others said she was murdered. In her car at a traffic light on 14th. At the laundromat on Ponce covered in detergent. At the IHOP on Clairmont in the ladies room covered in syrup.

What the hell? Was she even dead? I did not reply to any text, instead opted to text her directly — if I could find her number in my phone. I finally found it and sent a text: Hey, give me a call. I got a reply within a few minutes: *Who this?*

It's Adman.

You have the wrong number.

My bad. I'm sorry.

She changed her number. Damn it. Or maybe she didn't change it; just didn't want to talk to me. I can't blame her. It was ten years ago. I was drunk. My hangover had made a huge mess on her carpet…that I did not help clean. An old Jazz Cat I knew heard of the incident — we all gossip like old ladies — and gave me some advice.

One late night at a jam, he silently fingered his sax on the sidelines while a lady from the audience was singing *New York, New York* and *Happy Birthday To Me* for her girlfriends. He crooked a finger at me and said, "Come over here, Adman. I'm gonna help you out with the ladies. I've been watching you roll from one bed to the next, but never the same bed twice in a row. Why do you think that is, boy?"

I went to answer and he held up a finger. "Rhetorical question, boy. I don't need you to say a word because I know the answer. You just need to listen to ol' Rodney Wayne Manley." I nodded my head and he continued. "Ain't no good woman gonna put up with not being remembered. And they definitely don't like bad manners like throwing up on their carpet. You feel me, boy?"

I nodded some more. "So, you just listen to me. Got to stop it with all that stupidness you be doing. You might think you're a good lover, but if your alcohol-fueled playing is anything like your performance in the sack, well, I feel damn sorry for them ladies and I do not blame them at all for avoiding you."

Of course, I was stupid and didn't listen to him right away, but that was already too late for Harley Rose and me. Was she dead or alive? I had no way of finding out. It was too early to be up, so I turned off my phone and went back to bed. When I woke up at two, the sun was still bright but like it should've been and I was thinking much clearer about the situation. After my phone booted up, I punched in the numbers for my very best friend in the whole world. If anybody knew what was happening with Harley Rose, it would be Misha.

He didn't answer. Voicemail. Then I remembered: He was teaching. So I hung up and texted him: *What's up with Harley Rose?*

Forty minutes later, my phone rings. It's Misha. Oh, boy. I fully expected to find out reports of her death were wildly exaggerated. Even after all these years, his Russian accent was still as thick as ever. I've learned how to listen to him, though. It's a talent I've got for picking out the melody in a horn performance on stage that resembles a rude public chicken-choking party. When Misha gets all excited in English, I deploy that same talent in picking out the words which tell the story.

Misha was more excited than ever.

"Jaahhnn!" He always called me by my first name. Refused to use my nickname. Hated it when I called him The Russian Rocket. He'd say *My nim iss Meeshah!* Okay, okay, I'd say, *ne poluchay trusiki v povorote*. Even though that was my only Russian phrase I knew besides *nyet*, he hated it when I used Russian with him.

"Jaahhnn, you weel noat beleef. Harley Rose was murdered."

"For real? You ain't kiddin'?" I sat hard on my sofa.

"Yes, for re-al. So, I tell you what happen?"

"Yes," I said and took Sweet Stella off from around my neck and laid her on the sofa.

"Ohkaay. I tell you. So, she foun' Piedmont Park. Clothes all gone off her. Thrown all over."

"Damn. Raped and murdered."

"No! No-no. No rape. Fake-uh… ummm…you know…when crime scene made look like sumteen else…errrr…"

"Staged?" I said.

"Yes! Staged."

"How do you know all this?"

"*Eto glupyy vopros,*" he said, and I knew exactly what he meant. That was a stupid question because, while Misha was not Mafia or KGB or whatever they called themselves these days, he was from the Old Country and knew how to keep his ear to the ground. "So, staged crime scene. She haf note ohhn bohdy.

Eet say she not nice girl and get what she haf cohmink to her."

"Piedmont Park? That's right behind RLC. I don't remember seeing her there last night."

"You get there, she gone, but her car still at Red Light."

"Really? That means she had to leave with someone else or walk down the hill and up the steps into the park. I've never known her to leave her car and she would not walk all alone in that part of town, not in the dark."

"*Eessa tayna*…mystery."

"Jesus —" I started to say but was interrupted by the ever-joking Misha.

"I am not Savior. I am Meeeeesha."

"Ha. Ha. Listen. Think about it. She had to leave with somebody she knew. Which means we probably know the guy who killed her."

This did not impress Misha, as he had already thought of that. I knew he had already thought of that because his next comment was, "Well, duh." Delivered in perfect Southern dialect. Oh, he was a fun guy.

"How was she killed?"

"Nine mil. One, head. One, heart."

"Jesus."

Even Misha didn't have a joke for that. After a short contemplative silence, I told Misha I'd see him later at his place, and we disconnected.

We were booked into a series of venues around the Southeast and would end with a big final blowout in Atlanta, an extended special show, so rehearsals were in order. We were still working out our setlists as well as firming up singers who would be on-stage with us in each city. When we toured, Misha and I never traveled with female singers in tow. They slowed us down and were expensive to boot. If they made their own travel plans and were willing to pay for those, then more power to them, but we did not encourage that. We kept expenses down, and profits up, by booking singers local to the venue we were playing in. Less woman drama in our personal lives, too.

When we were younger, we were hound dogs like all the rest, but now it was just too much trouble. I had never married and, as the old joke goes, had no children I knew about. But Misha had just divorced his third wife and had a kid to support. No time to play around and tired of the gamble.

We had lots of details to work out, too. Which songs could the singers do well? What were their keys for each song? What were the feels, tempos, and timings they wanted to do them in? Which of those songs would fit into our double set and where? Which venues had pianos — and were they tuned —

and for which did Misha need to bring his keyboard?

The audience had no idea how much work went into putting on a show. They came to be entertained while they ate their meal and drank their drinks. Our goal was to always be so good they would want to listen and thus produce as little audience noise as possible.

Make no mistake about it, we put on a show. Shows and jams are two different animals, a fact performers are losing sight of these days. Showing up was only part of the equation. I was happy to work with Misha because he was just as anal retentive as I was. We weren't afraid of paperwork.

We kept two copies of each show. One on iReal Pro, an extremely helpful chart app accessed via smartphone or tablet. And if technology let us down, which can happen, we had two hard copies of each chart we could whip out and keep going.

After disconnecting from Misha, I thought I'd get back to shedding, but somehow I couldn't quite work up any enthusiasm for it. I knew what I needed. Got in my car. Took North Druid, passed Toco Hills, and turned left at LaVista and right on Briarcliff. Waikikie Hawaiian BBQ was on the left. I ordered ten wings, lemon pepper, and a double order of Spam Musubi. To go. But damn if it didn't smell so good in there that I ended up sitting at an outdoor table and eating every last bite.

I think that was good for me. The cold wind and the flavors perked me up and by the time I got home, I was in a shedding mood.

I felt sorry for Harley Rose, but her murder was not the first this city had seen nor would it be the last. I wouldn't miss her, not really, but now I could say

I now knew someone who had been murdered. A small bragging right, to be sure. Harley Rose deserved a requiem. I gave her one in my living room: Ruth Amy Norris, this one's for you.

3 Adman and Misha Prepare for Tour

One week had passed since Harley Rose was murdered, then another and another. The police were no closer to finding out who did it than they were when Harley Rose's body was discovered. There's an axiom in law enforcement: If you don't know who committed the murder within the first forty eight hours, then you probably never will. Forty percent of homicides go unsolved; it looked like my onetime lover was to be in that percentile.

Misha and I had two weeks left before we set out on our ten-day Southeastern tour. I spent my days on the phone, calling and texting and emailing singers, venues, hotels, and so forth. Firming up the details. At one time I had a booking manager, but that didn't last too long — don't get me started on why I fired him.

I set up an email address that simply said BookingAdman@gmail.com and a checking account with Booking Agents Ltd. as the company name. Sounded British and impressed some folks. Those took care of the business end, booking and collecting, while still leaving me free to play the star. That is a tip I picked up from an entertainment attorney one night in Los Angeles who was so drunk he was giving away advice for free. "Aaajjj*mon,*" he slurred, "if yer da stah, den be da stah. If yer goan be da money, den be dah money. But doan be da stah and da money. You loosh evah time."

Retentive, anal; me. In any case, things went smoother after I brought all the business details in-house and this tour was shaping up nicely. So there I was, ass deep in tour details and shedding, when my phone starts blowing up again. Another murder. Of someone I knew.

This time, though, it wasn't a past lover of mine that was murdered. It was Sam Lorenzo, composer, pianist. Found nude in plain sight on The BeltLine. Scattered around him were his clothes but also torn pieces of his compositions, sheet music, with words written in red permanent marker. Together the words read: Bad man. Got what he deserved.

Sam Lorenzo was an okay guy. We disagreed about music approaches. I am more the type that leads heart and soul. It wasn't that Sam played badly. Technically, the man had chops. If you were looking for somebody to do a same piece exactly the same way each time, he was the machine to do it. A technician. But Sam had no depth to his playing. Add that to the fact that he didn't know how to share the moment if that moment went outside the bounds of the standard, then you can see why a live Jazz environment was not where he needed to be.

But geez, to be murdered? Nah.

Live music with a small group on a stage is a different animal than a large ensemble. Jazz was outside his comfort zone, but he truly didn't want it to be, so I had to give him credit, he tried to stretch. But now he never would get that opportunity again.

Two people. Murdered. Both in the Jazz community. Both in Atlanta. Both with the same note. Had to be the same guy doing the dirty deeds. My gut knew there would be a third and maybe more.

You know what they say. One is a tragedy. Two is a coincidence. But three is a pattern. I've got this innate sense for all things evil. I understand the criminal mind. I can walk into any venue and immediately know if the owner/

manager is going to cheat me. Just as sure as I am of that, I was just as sure about there being more murders of people I know. So what motivates this person? Was it a fan? Was it a fellow musician? A singer? A songwriter? A show promoter? A venue owner?

What did Harley Rose and Sam Lorenzo have in common besides the Jazz world? Had he and Harley Rose been lovers? I didn't want to think about having shared a woman with him. I much preferred not knowing who the other men were in a woman's intimate life. Still, that upped the possible murderer pool, didn't it?

It was time to head over to Misha's and rehearse. I felt comfortable there. His entire living room was a studio. Grand piano on one side of the room. Vaulted ceiling with speakers built in and connected to a real organ. Computer. Mixer. Mics. And his dog,

Clutch, a male mongrel smart as a whip with personality to match.

When I arrived I could tell Misha was ready for a chat. After all, two people we both knew had been murdered within the space of three weeks. And Clutch wanted a good belly rub and tail scratching. I obliged both as we sat at the kitchen table drinking a cup of coffee.

Having grown up in the Soviet Bloc, Misha was well-versed in the existence of intrigue. But being an innocent at heart, he didn't understand it and soon was out of his depth. That's why he was never considered an enemy of the state. He tended to focus solely on the victims from his point of view. He didn't realize that Evil has its own interpretation that doesn't fit into normal, typical, regular thinking. Misha, so brilliant on the piano, was totally so normal I often wondered how we got to be such good friends. Well, maybe what he saw in me were all the things I missed in myself.

Anyway, he got lost when it came to understanding why these two were victims of such abnormal and dysfunctional psychological pathology, and no amount of explanation sufficed. So with chat over and belly rub and coffee finished, we got down to rehearsals. Three hours later we finished for the day. We walked out to my car. Me to leave. Misha to walk Clutch.

"I think I'll go to Kat's tonight," I said.

"I may see you," Misha said. "I may not. Depends."

I scratched Clutch's ears and said *Dazzagoodboy* in that way he likes and makes his tail wag, got in my car and drove away.

4 Adman Goes To Kat's

Kat's was a little club in Midtown Atlanta. Parking was a bitch, but there were plenty of folks who lived within walking or easy biking distance who didn't have to worry about it. So the club stayed packed on weeknights with customers buying drinks and pizzas, wraps, and — *shudder!* — salads, or what I called rabbit food. I found a parking deck, got my ticket, and drove up to E Level.

Before getting out of the vehicle, I secured my holstered Glock inside my front waistband and pulled my shirt down over it. Exited the vehicle. Got my case from the backseat. Slung straps over my shoulders. Locked doors. And walked confidently down flights of stairs and onto the street and the three blocks to Kat's.

Nobody but Misha and my woman knew I packed. Georgia was a carry state. Lots of people assumed that meant concealed carry, but they were wrong. It's just that gun folks in Georgia are polite. None of us want to flaunt our Second Amendment rights in front of bad guys and scaredy-cats. So, we conceal politely so as not to freak out certain folks.

Who was it that said *The best defense is a good offense?* Some football coach, if I remember correctly. How it is folks can understand that concept in a damn game but not understand it when it comes to their personal safety is beyond me. I do not apologize for this. You know me, I am opinionated and you might not agree.

It didn't take me too long to get to Kat's. The talk all evening was about the two murders. People were disturbed about it. Lots of theories. Lots of rumors.

Everyone also agreed the murders weren't random and that they had to be committed by somebody we all knew. Everybody was looking at each other crosswise when they didn't think the other was looking. It wasn't a good evening, but I did my best to soothe frayed nerves with my music.

A songwriter I knew showed up. Her name was Ruby Grace. As usual she brought a new song. I loved playing with her because she was always surprising and I liked surprises. My history with women made that plain. She loved it when musicians made her song their own in their solos or when they caught on quick to what she was trying to do and then supported that to turn the song into something even she could not imagine. Making magic live and in-person — no condom needed — was my personal taste of freedom with no worries.

There I was at the bar, nursing my usual, when up Ruby came. On the stage, she used my nickname Adman because that was marketing. But she always called me by my first name when she spoke directly. I loved how she said my name. She was Southern to the core and it came out lilting and melodic.

"Hello, JAH-aahhn."

"Ruby, my love. How are you?" I wrapped my arms around her and pulled her close, whereupon we kissed on the lips. We both knew we would never be lovers — she was married happily and faithfully — but we also knew that if she wasn't married we'd be all over each other in a Hotlanta minute.

She turned sideways, slid an arm around my neck, and grinned. "Why, ah am doin' juss fiiine, suh."

"Woman, you keep laying that thick Southern Belle on me and Imma gonna forget yer married."

She laughed. "You boys are so easy. So. You up for a new song tonight?"

"Hell yeah."

"Well, here. Let me send you the chart real quick. It's not too hard." She winked and grinned. We both laughed. She whipped out her phone and ding went my text notification. "There ya go. Toot-sweet fast. Just for you."

I downloaded the chart into iReal Pro and saved it to her playlist. Yeah, I saved all her stuff in a separate playlist because she was that good. When I got to be old and toddled up to a stage, I would want people to remember that I played her stuff when it was brand new. I opened the chart and she proceeded to sing the parts to me and let me hear how she was going to do it.

"This is where I think you can really have some fun with it. Right here. At the bridge." She pointed to the Dm, E^{b}, and G. Even danced out how her body would move when she sang it. She didn't go full Disco on me, but damn, that woman could cock a hip and say more than most strippers could on a stage with sawbucks being waved in their hoo-hahs. Among other ideas, that gave me lots to think on for musical interpretation.

Ruby's new song was dark. It was called *Black Roses Hang.* The lyrics from the bridge were –

In sleep I am aware.
Is this why I dream?
Perception is reality.
Is this why I scream?
Tell me why I am here.
Identity is strange.
Faith is not truth.
Black Roses hang.

I asked Ruby what they meant. She said whatever I wanted them to mean. I said but yeah how did you think them up? She said that's what she does: Think 'em up. I said her mind was a dark place. She said you have no idea. We laughed. But she wasn't the murderer. Not that a woman couldn't have done these because a woman certainly could. But not Ruby. Her darkness wasn't hidden. She used it for good. But this did bring up a good point.

Was our murderer a woman?

I thought on that as Ruby walked away and went to a piano player to see if he wanted to play on her tune. I watched as he quietly freaked out and she said don't worry and went in search of another. She finally found a young piano player who'd be willing to try it out. I watched as she went through the whole routine of sending him the chart, singing it through, and then pointing to me. I nodded my head when Wesley looked over at me. He turned back to Ruby, ready to go. He sent the chart to Landis, a bass player, who with one look committed it to memory. He would follow Wesley anyway. But the drummer did not get the chart. No need. Chet was so good that he'd catch on before the fifth bar started. I had a quick word with Kat and told her what we were going to do and who was going to do it. She let the bandleader know to make it happen.

And just like that Ruby had her quartet all lined up. We waited until we were called and then proceeded to blow the top off the joint. It was almost midnight.

Misha never did show up.

5 Adman and Misha Go On Tour

I went to Misha's and we loaded up my van, stopped off at the gas station, and fueled up. Misha scrubbed the windows and squeegeed off the water and dirt while I watched the filler nozzle until it popped and pumping ceased. We went inside, got some coffee, and then we were on the road. Our tour would start in Birmingham, so we hit I-20 W and put her into the wind.

"You know whazz we shoodo? Shood built sleeper rocks for…" he hooked a thumb toward the back of my van. "Saff lozz mohney."

"Damn, son," I said in my best Foghorn Leghorn voice. "I thinks, why I thinks you might just have a mighty fine, I say a mighty fine, idee."

Misha looked at me like I had lost my mind. "Whazz…why…you voice do…dat?"

"Sorry, I forget that even though you have been in America for well over twenty years, that you missed all the classic childhood cartoons. That was Foghorn Leghorn." Misha stared. "Never mind. However, I believe you think we should build a couple of sleeper racks in the back. It's a great idea. It's not like we'll be entertaining, so amenities be damned."

And so the rest of the miles to Birmingham went by as we discussed the project. We could rent showers at truck stops and shave in the shower. We ate out all the time anyway, so no cooking was needed, but we could get a large Coleman ice chest for drinks and other snack things. There were gas stations open twenty-four-seven with clean bathrooms. We had dental picks and such as that. Just as we hit the B'Ham city limits Misha already had the entire thing drawn up on paper, and to scale, as well as a list of materials we would need. I was to leave all the planning to him. The beds would fold up to load and unload, and at night we would fold them down and sleep.

Sounded good to me. I liked doing projects like that.

After Birmingham (two shows and two singers), we headed to Montgomery (one and two), then to Mobile, Tallahassee, and Jacksonville (one and one each), Savannah (two and three), Athens (one and one), then back to the Big ATL for a show at Red Light Café where we did a one-nighter with four singers and packed the place.

I tell you this: Me and Misha were slap worn out, but we had made some decent money. On our next tour, we would make even more because our expenses were going to be almost nil comparatively.

While we were gone, not once did I think of the murders. Didn't get any messages about them or any notification of new murders either, so no news is good news.

Eight days. Ten shows. Nine venues. Fifteen female singers. No roadies so we loaded in and out ourselves. Free drinks and food on show nights, but that ran the gamut from microwaved mozzarella sticks dipped in warmed-over tomato paste to burnt burgers with halfhearted fries. This life of ours is not easy. If I could choose something else, I would.

Once when I was younger I tried doing something else, but quickly found out my mind couldn't stay on the plucked chickens going by, swinging by their legs. If I hadn't been wearing a chainmail glove, I would've cut my hand off plenty of times. So, I figured in for a penny, in for a pound. Or as an old musician once told me, "You just got to make up your mind to step in it and step in it good."

He was right. I haven't looked back.

In any case, I spent the next three days sleeping except for the second day when a text dinged through to my consciousness. It was my woman saying she was bringing over lunch and I was to be up and presentable by the time she arrived. Which was in one hour. I showered, shaved, brushed my teeth, put on sweatpants and a wifebeater t-shirt. Threw on a light zip-up jacket and stuffed my toes into socks. Just in time. I could hear her drive up. I met her at the door and took two bags for her.

"Put those on the kitchen counter where the microwave is. Thank you," she commanded.

Damn, I love it when she gets mean. And she was mean today. I did as I was told and leaned up against the counter. She whipped around to me and said, "Well? Aren't you going to take them out of the bags?" I got busy. Hey, I knew marching orders when I got them. She turned and unpacked something that looked complicated. She turned on the oven, slid some glass dishes in, set the timer for one hour. Then gave me that look.

Oh, you know that look. That look that says *Do I have to tell you everything to do?* And I gave her that look that said *No ma'am, you do not.* After which I backed her up to the counter and proceeded to say hello in a proper manly-man fashion. We carried the hello to the back of the house where the bed was already untidy; she didn't give me any grief about my housekeeping at that moment, though she was mean to me and boy howdy was she ever. But, hey, I like it like that.

It's a good thing she set the timer on the oven because otherwise our food would've burnt.

6 Adman's Woman

I know you want to know my woman's name, but I will not tell you. See, she and I have a deal. We agreed on it upfront almost from the very first get-go. She didn't want to be Girlfriend of Public Figure. She would not come to my shows. No pictures of us would ever be on social media. Our families and friends would not know anything about us. She was not giving up her job. She would not follow me on the road. Here's what I will tell you about her.

She lives alone. No ex; well, no ex-husband. No children. No siblings. Parents are dead. Sounds sad. But she is smart and sexy and takes no prisoners. Works as a paralegal in a high-flying firm. Does not want to live together until such time, and only if it should happen, that we would make our relationship official by the filing for and getting a marriage license. Older than me but not by much. Doesn't like emotional holidays that prey on softhearted wimps to get them to spend money. Which suits me just fine. She told me, "Don't you ever buy me a present because some ad campaign told you it was time to do so. Don't get me wrong, I like surprises. But not one dictated by advertising agencies. Furthermore, if we ever have sex, you best not be touching any other women. "

I simply stood there and stared. Then she said, "Well? We clear? You agree?" I nodded my head and fell in love. She would not be a budget-buster, that's for sure. I liked a practical woman. However, after a couple of years of that, I told her that I wanted to take our relationship to the next level. Yes, boys and girls, I wanted to put a ring on it. She wasn't ready for a wedding ring, so we compromised and made it an engagement ring. And so with the on-my-knee asking for her hand and her acceptance of that offer, a ring was chosen and placed upon her finger with all the smiling and champagne-cork-popping one could ever wish for.

But we are committed one to the other and never a straying shall occur and, frankly, I am so much calmer now. I've got me somebody. She's mine and I'm hers. We worry about each other and help each other. And we don't do it for public consumption. And that makes me happy. We've been together five years and it's been the best five years of my life. It's nice not to have to worry about emotional imbroglios. Drama is not for me.

So that's all you need to know about my lady.

7 Adman Goes to Joe's

A few days later I spent a couple of days at You Know Who's house. She had a honey-do list and I liked being bossed around by her, so naturally it was a good fit. We went to the big-box stores and bought nails and hooks and other stuff to repair and build. We had a good weekend. She cooked and pointed. I ate and said Yes Ma'am. But come Monday it was time to get back into the groove and I did.

First stop was in my living room to say hello to Sweet Stella. A little bit of shedding and laundry and other household chores took up most of Monday and Tuesday. But on Tuesday evening my case and I showed up at Joe's Jazz Jam. Everybody wanted to know where I'd been. Told them I'd been on tour. They wanted to know how it went. Told them it was fine.

Headed back to the bar where the new girl had no clue what my usual was, but I finally got it and stood in the back looking at the tables to see where there might be an opening where I could sit with folks I knew. But tonight it was mostly strangers, so I took myself to a corner near the stage. Joe was blowing hard, but when he turned around and saw me his horn popped up and down in acknowledgement and his eyebrows arched up in *You wanna come up next?* I nodded and unpacked.

Joe and the house band and the singer finished to big applause. Joe went up to the microphone and did his thing.

"Thank you. We enjoyed doing that song. Hey, give a big hand for Mari. Didn't she do a great job with that Mancini song? [Clap, clap, clap!] Yeah. Hey, look who's here. Adman, you want to come up? Give the Adman a big hand everybody. Hey, long time no see. Where you been? [I hollered *tour.*] Oh-ho! He's been on tour. Well, glad to have you back in town."

Joe called up a singer, too, then counted it off and before you knew it, we were having some fun with *Life Is A Funny Old Broad* in B minor, the singer's key. I got plenty of time for solos as did the rest of the band. We went around the world with that tune in almost twenty five minutes and never once lost that audience's attention. We traded fours and I swear we all got lost toward the end until finally Joe blew in our ears and reoriented us to the big finale. But the audience didn't seem to care because we were having such fun and they went right along with us.

That was fun. I got off the stage, stowed Sweet Stella in its case, and walked back to the bar. Found an empty seat. Felt a tap on my shoulder and turned around. Damn. I couldn't recall his name but he played guitar…he was alright.

"Hello, Adman. How you d-d-doing, man?"

"Hey, man," I said and held out my hand for shaking. "What's up? Did you play tonight?"

"Yeah. Early in the evening. I d-d-didn't see you."

"Oh, man. Sorry I missed it. I didn't get here until a little after nine. How you been doing?"

"Oh, I'm d-d-doing fine. Much better, in fact. Been under some s-s-stress, though, but you know, what doesn't k-k-kill you makes you s-s-stronger, right?"

We both got a good laugh out of that. I said, "That is what I hear anyway. Hey, this stress, I hope it isn't something with your health."

"N-n-noo, no, no. Not my health. Just some interpersonal shit I got t-t-to take c-c-care of. You know how it is."

I nodded. "That I do, my friend. That I do. Listen, if you need to talk sometime, just let me know."

"Thanks, Adman. I appreciate the offer. You know, you're one of the n-n-nice ones. I l-l-l-ike you," he said, putting a hand on my shoulder in a friendly sort of way. "Just remember that, okay? I l-l-ike you."

"I will remember."

"It was g-g-good to see you, Adman."

"Same here."

Then he turned on his heel, stalked to the corner where he stowed his case, slung it over his shoulder, and stalked out the door.

Poor guy. What was his name? Started with an R…I think.

8 Adman Gets a Letter

It had been so long since the last murder that I'd already lost count of the days and hadn't been thinking about it as much either. I hit Red Light Café late Wednesday evening for the J Nick Jazz Jam there. It usually got started around nine but I liked to get there around half-past ten or a little later. Mitchie was packing up the door early. We chatted briefly and he waved me on in. The students had usually gone home by ten-thirty, what with early classes the next day. If the Jazz Cats that showed up were a good mix, then sometimes they'd been known to play until almost one.

Michael saw me coming. He held up a finger and arched his brow in *Your usual?* and I nodded in the affirmative. The crowd was pretty light. It seemed the mood wasn't right for much collaborative improvisation. Nobody knew where J Nick was. He was the bandleader who ran this jam; he was always there unless he was at a large Jazz festival, so everybody was worried. I was out the door by twelve.

Thursday night I bopped over to Decatur and popped in at the Drunken Bird Grill and Bar. The house band's drummer did a riff and they all hollered *Adman!* and went on with their set. There were maybe fifteen people watching. Six were holding their horns and two were singers I recognized. Waving and nodding, I went to the bar and ordered a Three Taverns Rapturous and house wings with fries and found a seat for me and my case.

The piano player picked up the mic. "Good evening, ladies and gentlemen. Welcome to the Pop Up Jazz Jam at Drunken Bird. Happy you've joined us this evening. We've got some horns here to play and I see a couple of singers, too. And we've got the Adman in the house tonight. How you doing, Adman?"

Hollering back at him, "I'm hungry!"

Everybody laughed. "Yeah, well, whatcha wanna bet your food comes out just as I call you up?" More laughter from everybody and nods and grins from me. He turned toward a singer. "Okay, darlin'? You ready to sing? Great. Come on. Whatcha wanna do?"

Song title and key given, I settled back to listen and wait on my food. And a little while later, sure enough, just as I got started on a song, out came my food. Big laughs. But hey, when you're hungry, you'll eat even if it's cold.

Friday morning found me being woken by texts coming in hot and heavy. Man, what's the matter with people sending texts so early? Somebody better have died or I was going to be pissed. Cursing but finally managing to focus my eyes, I said *Shit!*

It wasn't morning.

It was two in the afternoon.

And somebody had died.

Been murdered, to be more precise. J Nick was found in his home. He'd been dead since late Sunday night. A note like the others was on the scene. Well, that explained why he had not shown up at Red Light Café Wednesday night, requiring somebody else to volunteer as bandleader. Seems his ex-wife got worried and went looking. He didn't answer phone or door — which he always did if it was her calling or visiting, even if he was boinking some star-struck woman.

She called the police for a wellness check. One officer pulled himself up to look into a high window at the back of the house and saw the body.

At least that's what the scuttlebutt was saying.

Well, crap. I wondered what would happen to the Wednesday night jam. I texted Michael to see if he had heard anything. He texted back *You wanna run it?* I said I'd think about it. *Let me know quick because Wednesday isn't far away.* I said I'd run it Wednesday and we'd talk about long-term later.

Sad really. We're all replaceable. We take our showers. We put on our suits du jour. We comb our hair and brush our teeth and practice, practice, practice and people clap and sometimes give us money and for what? To be replaced that quick?

I wondered what J Nick would think about getting traded in so easily. Knowing him, his ego would be bruised. But hey, he was in the big sleep now and didn't know a thing. My email dinged incoming. Hellll*oooo*. An online lesson was scheduled through a booking service I used. Hey, money's money. I put it on my calendar and set a reminder ding for it. Now it was time to get my house band together for Wednesday at RLC, our shorthand for Red Light Café.

I was thinking Misha on piano, but he had a regular gig at another restaurant every Wednesday and it definitely paid more, so with child support as a budget line item, he wasn't about to trade in a favor for hard cash.

Jams don't usually pay too much, even to the house band itself. But jams serve a purpose: They are good paid practice sessions for them. I go to jams to check out up-and-coming talent, see who's still around, network, and so forth. Running the jam meant I could put into play some ideas I have, but doing it regularly wouldn't be a huge moneymaker, for sure.

Michael updated his social media and website to reflect my running of the jam next week. I shared those links. Then I sent out an email blast to my fans to let them know about it. Hoped the jam with me as head would draw a crowd. Then I lined up a bass player, drummer, and keys. A bit of excitement was in store. It had been years since I had done it. I had something to look forward to.

Before I knew it, the day had passed, no more news of murders had arrived, and the evening was upon me. You Know Who was coming over. We were going to cook a late dinner and watch a movie. I saw her headlights sweep across the front of the house when she turned in and I was out in the driveway doing my best tail-wagging meet-and-greet happy dog routine. She scratched my belly like I scratched Clutch's and said — I swear — *Whooozzagootboy-*

Yewwzzagootboy. In any case, I smiled and carried what she gave me.

"Did you check your mail today?" she asked.

"I did not."

"I'll go get it," she said. I watched her walk to the mailbox at the street and get out a pile of stuff. "John, how long since you checked your mail?"

I thought about it and couldn't remember. "Never mind," she said. "We'll go through it later."

"Yes, ma'am."

Whooozzagootboy? Yewwzzagootboy-yesssyouare.

The evening went fine and we went to bed and fell asleep like an old married couple. Upon waking in the morning to a pup tent, she was already cooking breakfast, so my tent fell and I went out to a big breakfast and a good-morning kiss followed by *It's ready. Sit.* I sat and ate.

She was going through my mail. Circulars and coupons and junk went straight to the trash can she had moved to be next to her. Catalogs of gear were stacked for me to look through later. Bills went in another stack. Then there was one pile that couldn't really be called a pile because it had one hand-addressed letter with no sender name or return address.

"What's that?" I asked.

"Don't know. Addressed to you."

I stared at it for awhile. Personal written correspondence sent through the United States Postal Service was not something I got any kind of regular.

"It won't bite," she said and handed it to me. I looked it over. Mailed from Marietta, or Maaay-rhetta if you prefer. "Open it, for God's sake."

"Okay! Okay! You don't have to nag me about it." I peeled the flap apart and saw four handwritten sheets. Lined notebook paper. Pencil. I flipped to the last page to see who had sent it, but all it said at the end was

Sincerely, Your Friend

I started reading. Got through the first page of rambling with seemingly no point then almost jumped out of my skin halfway down the second page.

"Holy shit!" I hollered.

"What?" You Know Who shouted.

I stood up and cleared a spot at the end of the table, laying all the pages out using just the tips of my fingers. "I think this is a letter from the killer of my friends."

She stood. We put our heads together and bent over to read it together. She read it out loud. Here's what it said:

Dear Adman,

I want to think you for beng friend. You always ben nice to me and I appreciate that. You have nothing to fear from me. Ever. I mean it. I swear. But some folks in this world don't know the pain they visit upon me regular and don't have to when they could just as easy be frindly and we could all get along but they don't be nice and they don't smile and thy always putting me down and insulting me and saying bad things and it's just not right.

I know you agree with me on this because I've seen how you

look at them when they get mean and catty and koi and I seen how you don't like it when they try to drag you in on there putdowns.

That's right. I seen you stand up for the little guy and I know I'm a little guy don't mean much in this world but even little guys got to be treated nice cuz there ain't no cause or reason for it otherwise. But do they learn there lesson? Know they don't. They miss every nice thing you do and just act like the mean fuckers that they are.

So I had to do something I tell you I had to do something and I couldn't wait no longer. Lessons had to be taught and maybe somebody would learn from those lessons but not the ones I teach it to because they are dead.

I know you agree that them dying is the best thing I know you do and I want you to know I value your support in my mission. Harley Rose might sing like a songbird, but her heart is cold as ice and mean as a junkyard dog and evil as a double-headed rattler even though the rattler is just doing what comes natural the way God intended. But God did not intend her to be like that. And God didn't intend Sam Lorenzo and J Nick to be mean either. Don't they see music is supposed to heal not tear apart no they don't see that they use it as a weapon to destroy, enslave, trick

They are taking what God gave them their beautiful talent for making music as he intended and they are using it for evil evil evil evil evil evil evil evil evil evil evil evil evil evil

The rest of the letter pretty much said the same thing but a little different. We went to my computer where she sat in front and searched for who was leading this case. There were three counties so maybe it was the GBI. She finally found a name associated with a police department, looked her up, and found her number. I called. While we waited, my lovely, smart fiancé took closeup pictures of each page.

"Why are you doing that?" I asked.

"In case some idiot loses the actual letter," she said.

"Damn, woman. You are so smart."

Ding-ding-ding-ding went my text tone. Four pictures arrived. "Backup for our backup." She looked up at me. "When did they say they'd be here?"

I grinned. "Two hours."

She grinned. It was time to go make a pup tent again.

Two hours later two female detectives were at my house taking the letter and envelope as evidence. They snapped on gloves and put each sheet and the envelope into separate plastic bags and sealed them. We sat around the dining room table. They read the letter and we talked about the contents. They wanted to know who wrote me. I said I had no idea. Didn't recognize the handwriting. Didn't recognize anything.

Had no clue why anyone would send me a letter and didn't they have people who could figure that stuff out by the use of handwriting analysis and linguistics and shit like that?

One of them made a snarky comment under her breath about bureaucrats' budgets being a criminal's best friend. You Know Who's eyes turned to slits upon that comment and she stared hard at the detectives.

Then one asked why I was called Adman and I said it started years and years ago and was because I was always "advertising" my gigs and somebody made fun of me doing that and said I wasn't a real artist because I wanted to make money and next thing you know it stuck and I forgot who said that to begin with but he disappeared –

Disappeared? they interrupted, cocking their head and saying in unison *Like disaPPEARED?* I said *Not disaPPEARED disappeared, just left the scene, you know?*

After every question they both stared at me like I was lying, but that was just their natural resting faces so I wasn't worried.

They turned to You Know Who and boy did their attitude change. She had been sitting there making notes the whole time they had questioned me. Resting faces changed to polite inquiry and *if you please, ma'am*. She had nothing much to add other than it was she who checked her lazy fiancé's mail.

I had to go get fingerprinted so they could eliminate my prints from the letter. You Know Who had also handled the envelope so she had to get fingerprinted, too. We went together, right away, so the evidence could be properly processed, bureaucrats' budgets be damned.

We weren't considered suspects and she made sure that our fingerprints were to be used for elimination only and not kept on file.

God, my woman was a force of nature. I couldn't wait until we went public with our relationship. If she kept up this sort of awesomeness, I was going to have to push to break our deal of keeping quiet. And so it came to be that I lived up to my wild, creative, songwriting, musician, singer *artiste* roots on the way back to the house. I was driving and finally it all just came blurting out.

9 Adman Takes Advice from Inside Southern Man and Manly Commando

"Damn it all to hell, woman. A man can only take so much."

Of course, as soon as the blurt from this worldwide-known *artiste* was out, my Inside Southern Man spoke harshly to me: *Whut the hayle yew doin'?*

You Know Who said, "I know. That poor fella." Thank goodness she totally misunderstood my meaning and my hands relaxed on the steering wheel while my ISM said *Dodged a bullet there, you lucky sumbitch.*

"Wait. What poor fella?"

"The murderer."

"Why 'that poor fella'?"

"He said it all in his letter. Folks with no manners and arrogant attitudes pushed him past his limit. Isn't that what you were talking about?"

Watch what you say, you stupid sumbitch, ISM reminded me. "Oh, yeah. Yeah. Sure. Of course…he is a murderer…so I think there are more healthier ways to handle one's angsts and torments, aren't there?"

"Of course, sweetie. But still…"

I did not think this was going to be a good time to bring up my particular angst and torment nor give her any orders. ISM had a good idea: *Maybe take her out to dinner. Wine and dine her. Get her all relaxed and thinking nice and kind thoughts about you.*

"Hey, this has been a stressful day," I said. "What say I take you out to eat tonight? Somewhere special. Swanky, even. You know, where a man can wear jeans but he better have them pressed with a knife-edge crease along the front and have it all topped off with a jacket and tie. Whaddayasay?"

She laughed, but then got all practical on me. "Isn't that expensive?"

My hands gripped the steering wheel tighter. "Woman! I am a man. And if this man wants to take out his woman somewhere swanky and spend some damn money on her then, damn it all to hell, he can do that."

You Know Who turned her head back to the road and said, "Okay. What time shall I be ready?"

"Seven o'clock."

"I will be ready."

"Okay."

"Oooookaaaay." But she didn't say it snarky. She said it quiet and a little bit flirtatious and I took a quick look at her and saw she was smiling.

Well done, ISM said proudly.

We arrived back at my house and You Know Who got in her car to go to her house. She gave me a little wave. You know the kind. The little tips wiggling and blowing your way after having been kissed that somehow, magically, makes way to your heart and makes you smile. Yeah, that kind. I watched her car until it turned the corner and was out of sight, then looked at my watch. It was a little after four. I better hurry up if I was going to iron those sharp creases into my jeans.

Hell, I better find a restaurant and make a reservation, too. After several calls to eateries that did not feature live music — after all, I didn't want to run into anybody I knew while squiring a woman around — and everything being all booked up, I finally called Pastique and said I needed a reservation for two for this evening at eight. The man taking the reservations said fortune had smiled on me this day as he just had a cancellation for two at eight this evening and would I like to claim the spots. Why yes, yes I would.

Jeans, sharp and crisp, and tie chosen, I sent the pictures of the letter on my phone to my email, then logged onto the computer and printed them out full size. I thought I may as well study them for clues and read through them while enjoying a cup of coffee. There was something about the friend angle that kept my attention. Somehow that seemed important. Like I'd heard it somewhere recently. But it just wouldn't come to mind.

It was time to go, so I showered and shaved, brushed my teeth, got myself dressed, though I decided to go commando tonight. There was something ruggedly sexy about having the cloth of the jeans against bare manly parts. Tonight was going to be a commando night for sure. All my gumption was going to be needed for this conversation and commando would simply remind me that I was a man, damn it all to hell, and don't forget it.

I texted her I was on my way, which meant arrival would be in thirty minutes what with traffic and such. Like always, in her practical manner, she was outside on the porch waiting for me when I pulled up. She stood up slowly and swished her way to the vehicle. Manly Commando spoke up and when she slid into the vehicle and closed the door she leaned over for a kiss and I got a peek at her puppies at which point Manly Commando started barking orders – *Left! Left! Left-Right-Left!* Oh, my. You Know Who glanced at Manly Commando and said, "*Whooozzagootboy-Yewwzzagootboy.*"

We laughed, I put it in reverse, and off we went. We arrived with ten minutes to spare. Some other folks grumbled but hushed when the host said, "Sir, reservations are always seated first." I put my hand on the small of my woman's back and followed like a good boy as we were led to our booth. Menus were placed. A waiter helper came around, turned over glasses and filled them with water. Another helper placed a sliced, crusty, hot baguette and real butter on the table, along with two small plates. Along came the waiter who made grand introductions, learned our names, and took drink orders.

We sat side by side on a generously proportioned banquette, buttered our bread, and with first bites took a look around the place. It was all whites and shiny royal blues and everything rounded off. Not a sharp corner in sight unless you looked under the tablecloth to see the creases in my jeans. When You Know Who slid her hand from my knee to thigh, Manly Commando barked orders again just as our waitress came by and said, "May I give you tonight's specials of the kitchen?"

I couldn't speak, so just nodded, but You Know Who took her hand off my leg and said, "Ooooo. Yes, please."

After ten minutes of hearing reductions this and a-oilee that and green thing topped by crusty thing alongside elephant-something-or-the-other, I said, "Thank you. Can we think about all that and look at the menu for awhile?"

"Of course," she said, and backed away with a smile.

"What'd she say the specials were?"

My woman smiled and said, "Bunch of expensive frou-frou you won't like, so it doesn't matter. She sure did a good job of saying all that, didn't she? They usually rush through it, but she acted like she had a personal relationship with each dish and really, really, really cared about them."

We laughed at that and began perusing the menu. There were no pictures, so I had to read a lot and get guidance as to whether or not it would be something I would like. Finally, she said, "Babe. You like steak. Here." She pointed helpfully.

"Steak, potato, another side choice, and salad. Right up my alley."

Both our waiter (he was in training) and waitress came back to take our order. That took another ten minutes by the time we each said how we wanted everything. He came back to pour us more wine and we ate more bread. No fuss. No rush.

"So, babe," I began. "I'd like to talk to you about something."

She took a sip of wine and nodded.

"Okay, so, the thing is…we're engaged."

She nodded and bit her bread.

"And, frankly, I'm tired of not letting the world know about you."

She stopped chewing momentarily, her eyes went all squinty, then she resumed mastication. Rather, I should say, she was now grinding the bread between her teeth. So while her mouth was busy and she couldn't say anything, I kept on talking.

"Look, I know you got your reasons for wanting to be private and so forth, but I'm beginning to —"

And here is where ISM took over and went for the laugh.

"— well, I'm beginning to feel disrespected. Like I'm a Boy Toy or something."

Timing that just as she swallowed almost made her choke, but she was laughing all the same. "Boy Toy!" Her laughter rang out across the restaurant. Folks were turning toward us. This was not my idea of going public. "B-b-boy T-t-toy. Hahahaha! Haha-hahaha!"

My face was red. I pretended I wasn't there until she finally got it all together and sipped her wine.

"Stop making jokes and say what you really mean."

Oh, damn. I could hear that paralegal voice. I kept my mouth shut and silently recited *Oh, Lord. Grant me the serenity to accept the things I cannot change, the courage to change the things I can, and the wisdom to know the difference.* She just waited. I took two big gulps of wine for courage. Okay. Ready? Set? Go!

"Okay…I will...I…I want to get married. I want to live in the same house with you. I want to wear a wedding band in public. I want people to know I'm taken. I'm tired of hiding. So…you onboard with this or what?"

I sat back, picked up my wine, and stared straight at her. ISM was silent; we were awaiting for her reply.

"Huh. That is interesting."

Yep. That's all she said for awhile. We drank more. Ate more bread, then out came the simple salads; we waved away the pepper grinder. We grazed our way through those, and damn they were good, when out came the main courses. We ate some more. All you could hear were knives sawing and forks clanking and glasses setting and two people chewing and swallowing. I was not going to break the silence. This was Manly Commando time and, damn it all to hell, I was going to live up to that credo.

Ain't no woman gonna make me speak up first and lose the advantage. In this I was determined and set.

It took us all of thirty minutes to finish our meal. A dessert menu was laid in front of us and we were asked if we wanted any. I pointed to a chocolate something-or-'nother and then at coffee. The trainee waiter said, "Sharing the dessert? Two spoons?" I nodded again, still silent.

Helpers came and cleared away the plates and, using some sort of little brush, swept our table of pesky crumbs. Still, nothing from her…until, I felt her hand go to my knee. Oh, she wasn't going to play that game. Oh, no, no, no. I would not fall for that trick and Manly Commando agreed with me. We were hunkered down in our foxholes waiting for offer of armistice. This was not détente, baby, this was war.

Her hand moved up and patted my thigh. Manly Commando was under a mighty strain, but he endured the onslaught and did not cave.

Dessert came. We ate. Coffee was served. We drank. Bill presented. Paid.

Still nothing.

Valet brought the car. I tipped. We got in. I drove.

Still – nothing.

Until I pulled into her driveway and she said, "So, what you're saying is that you want to actually get married? Now? And live together? And all that stuff?"

"That is what I am saying."

She got her house keys out of her purse, jangled them a moment, then looked at me and smiled. "Well…okay."

"Okay? Okay? You mean yes to what I want?"

She nodded again.

"Whoohoo! Oh-kay!" I kissed her on the lips. She got out and walked to her front door and waggled those little kissed fingertips at me. I couldn't stop grinning and kissed my fingers and waved back at her.

She went inside and flicked the front porch light twice, our code for her to say she's all locked up, and I backed out the drive and went home.

Imma gonna git married.

ISM and Manly Commando both congratulated me on my victory.

10 Comes a Second Letter

The first thing I was going to do when I got home was Friend her on Facebook. Except she'd already beat me to it. And she had put In A Relationship as her status and tagged me as the one she was in it with. I let that show on my Timeline and commented under it: We're getting married. Details when we get them.

By mid-morning when I got up there were quite a few comments full of shock and good wishes and requests for the date. I heard from people I had forgotten about. The emoji that outstripped them all was the one with the laughing face, but lots of thumbs up and heart emojis too. After five hundred, I quit looking to see who had responded. Sheesh.

Anyway, three days later, here comes another letter from the murderer. I was just slicing envelopes open without looking at them. My mind was elsewhere, so paying attention was not first and foremost. But when I saw the handwriting, I said *rut-roh*. I put on some vinyl gloves I had in the toolbox, laid the sheets out, took pictures, and texted those to my woman, who texted back to call the detectives. I replied *yes ma'am* like a good affianced man should.

But not before I read the letter. This one was only two pages long. Here is the nut of what it said.

Dear Adman,

Saw you post on FB about getting married. Congratulations, man. I'm happy for you. I was married one *time, but it didn't last. We were together for six months when she died, I mean, disappeared.*

Hey Im sure your marriage will be happier than mine was. I hope to meet you financee one day. Maybe she'll come out to a jam one night and you can introduce us.

There was more, but nothing about any current murders. Geez. According to this, I knew the guy well enough to know his name and make introductions? Who did I know whose wife had disappeared?

Nobody I could think of.

I called the detectives and they were out in an hour. I had folded the letter and put it back in the envelope and said as soon as I saw who it was from I had called them. The inside handwriting was the same, but the outside writing was from a computer printout that was cut and taped on the front. Well, now they had the letter and they could get busy. They were excited about the big clue — his wife had disappeared — and questioned me about that. Again… nothing. With the letter pages and envelope in separate plastic bags, they took their leave.

I got busy practicing a new piece I'd been working on. An original song wherein I am experimenting with a four-bar repetition. The tune is written for piano. I know, my instrument for performance is sax, but I am fond of writing original tunes on piano.

There's more to play with on that instrument and it can carry all the pieces of a song much better than a saxophone or other instrument.

I have this repetition that I believe Ruby Grace would like to put words to, maybe even her own interpretation of melody over it. I sent her a text and told her what I had in mind for a collab. She texted back she was all in. I told her if she wanted to come over, I could show her what I've got so far and see what she thought. She agreed.

I texted her my address and we set a time for later that evening.

She arrived at 7:30. All grins and happy-happy congrats for upcoming nuptials.

"Hello, JAH-aahhn."

"Hey, darlin'. How yew doin'?"

"FYE-ann. But look at you. Getting married. Pretty quick turn of events, isn't it?"

"Nope. We've been together for five years and engaged for three."

"What? BAY-bee, you are a dark horse, ain't yew?"

"I am!"

I poured coffee and we sat at the piano and I played my experiment.

It was quite simple, really, musically speaking. The intent and power would come from the pacing, intensity of play variations, and so forth. Here's my idea:

Three-quarter time, so Waltz time for you non-music people.

Never-changing C minor chord played with the right hand. For non-music people that would mean play at the same time C, E flat, and G.

The left hand would play, in turns, C, B flat, A flat, and G.

So the whole tune consists of:

Hit a C on the one and hold. On the two and three hit the C minor chord.

Hit a B flat on the one and hold. On the two and three hit the C minor chord.

Hit an A flat on the one and hold. On the two and three hit the C minor chord.

Hit a G on the one and hold. On the two and three hit the C minor chord.

Looks simple, you're thinking. This isn't a Jazz song. Well, technically it isn't Jazz because the foundational chords may be so simple, but there is a method to my madness. Do you remember I told you earlier that I like experimentation? And do you remember that I like to give people opportunity to experiment with a foundational concept? Well, I might not've told you that, but isn't that what experimentation is? You take a foundation and mess with it?

Anyway, Ruby made notes and I played on the piano how it would go. She had me play it through while she recorded it on her Voice Memo. After almost two hours, she left with an "I'll work on it, sweet cheeks" and a wave, then off to hubby and home she went.

11 Adman's Hard Thoughts

Wednesday night I showed up to lead the band at the jam at RLC. It's all going good. We're having a lot of fun. Lots of young lions heard I'd be there and showed up to play, so it was horn-heavy, but the singers who showed up were happy to have them on-stage with them. Three guitars walked in. Two bass players. Four drummers. Well, sometimes you just got to let the band have its head and so that night we had some fun but totally never to be repeated performances.

Ruby showed up late, late, late. It was a little after eleven. I crooked my finger at her and she popped up on stage in the middle of a long drum solo. I whispered in her ear. She whispered in mine. We both nodded. Then I stepped over to Keys and whispered in his ear. He grinned and nodded at me, then at Ruby. She was close enough on the small stage to give him a hug. Drummer, even though the audience thought he was so totally into his own creation that he was not noticing anything else was, in point of fact, watching me and Ruby out of one slit eye. Bass didn't need to be told anything. He would catch on quick and lend all the support we would need. Yeah, he was that good.

Drum solo ended with the bass and keys and me and Sweet Stella playing the last eight bars and ending together to big applause. I stepped to the mic.

"Ladies and gentlemen, tonight we're going to debut a new song of mine. Ruby Grace, wonderful songwriter, put lyrics to it and we want to run it by you and see whatcha think about it so far. I've not yet heard them, so I'm going to get surprised just as much as you. And hey, for you musicians out there willing to fly by the seat of your pants," I pointed out to the horns and guitars, "you guys jump in when you get the drift. I don't have a title yet —"

Ruby said, "Darlin' JAH-aahhn. I've got a title I think you will like."

"Oh, yeah," I growled sexily into the mic. "Well then, tell us."

She nodded. "*Twisting In The Wind*. And Ja-AAHNN?"

"Yes, darlin'," I purred into the mic.

"You are gonna love it."

And we were off. We ended up playing that song for almost forty minutes. Keys had a variation he did on his solo. He and Ruby went back and forth on that, just teasing each other. Then Bass had a solo. Drum's solo was interesting, too. He'd already started catching on to Ruby's idea. Then she brought a…a…sensibility of…of… exposure, of baring the soul, that led everyone else to places they had not been. And no matter who had the variation, the others followed that lead. Even the audience got in on it. I heard moans of pleasure that sounded like "Oh, Geeeezus!" and "God Almighty" and a few other sounds that one cannot begin to tell because they belonged to that person in that moment along with not a few whistles.

So, it was a Jazz song after all, Acid Jazz…thanks to Ruby's lyrics spurring us on. And isn't that what Jazz is all about?

Communication. Listening. Sharing. Feeling. Speaking the same language. Telling the same story, often a sad one, from a different point of view. Being in the moment with others to whom you did not need to explain one thing because they got it. And thus ended the night with all us Cats — and Kittens — engrossed in mental chatter like Jimmy Miller and Steve Winwood sung about in their song *I'm a Man*. And the place stayed packed, so that was a big yay for us.

I know you're going to want to know what the lyrics are that Ruby wrote. So, hold onto your porkpie hats, boys and girls, because you are going to see the brilliance of her words right here and now. Talk about the dark side of love. Whew.

"You only live once,
so keep having fun"
are the words you
said to me.
You may be right,
and yes I do.
Still, your words,
they haunt me.

You say I'm

funny and
I make you laugh,
and we'll talk more
later on.
But later never comes
and I'm left
twisting
in the wind.

Fun isn't all it's
cracked up to be.
Substance must become
sweet reality

For me you have
a hunger. When you
sweet talk your
voice is soft and low.

You make me believe
I'm desperately wanted
and from your words
my desire grows. But
later never comes
and I'm left
twisting in the wind.

You're not here.
Now comes my fun.
I pour it all out
on other men.
They get my loving.
It breaks my heart.
I can't wait for them
to leave.
Oh, Oh, Oh,
twisting.

You're jealous of
temporary lovers
lighting up
my nights.
You're happy
they're gone,
your heart still wants me so —
or so you say.
Here I go again,
pouring myself
into you,
the one man I want
but can't seem to
have.

But later never comes
and I'm left
twisting in the wind.
OHHHH!

Love is a seed so the song goes.
And in the spring it becomes a rose.
Fun only cuts the heart open wide.
Soon it will be a large scar.

[Here, Ruby stopped the band with a hand gesture and went vocal only.]

Oh, I don't only want to be
just a fond memory
of what a man could
handle in his prime.

Oh-oh-oh, I

[Here, the band jumped in, kicking it to match her vocal lead.]

hate you.
Why did you ask me to dance?
I hate you.

Why did I take a chance?
I hate you.
Why did you make love so fine?
I hate you.
Why did I have to mind?

Can't get you out of
my mind,
no matter how many
times I'm left
twisting in the wind.

Fun isn't all it's
cracked up to be.
Substance must become
sweet reality.
Oh, oh, oh…
Twisting.
Twisting.
Twisting in the wind.
I.
Hate.
You.

And? Wow. Of course my first thought was "Did this happen to her?"

My second thought was "It doesn't really matter." Inspiration comes from many places and stories told can belong to another. She turned those lyrics upside down and around until they sounded like sad love, angry passion, grief-stricken regret, and a pleasure so painful she wouldn't trade it for a thing.

I could not have written such a story. Who was it years ago that wrote a song that said "come on, baby, make it hurt so good"? Well, that was our Jazz version of that theme. Damn, I was going to have to get Ruby and the band over to record. Why not a have a new release, right?

In any case, I was so pumped up with those happy hormones and adrenaline that I didn't manage to crawl in the bed and go to sleep until almost seven in the morning.

When I woke up it was late afternoon, almost four, and I said to myself *rut-roh.*

I've been living by myself and this schedule of mine — not being able to sleep all night and getting up and playing or watching television or cooking like I sometimes did — would interrupt my woman's sleep and she works during the day. Shit. I hadn't thought of that. Neither of us could change their schedule. I certainly couldn't, but, I mean, my woman could if she changed careers. But that wasn't going to happen.

I picked up the phone and texted her in all caps: CALL ME!

Her return text was: Is this a 9-1-1 CALL ME or an I've got an idea CALL ME? I replied: When you can. No hurry. She replied with a luscious lips kiss emoji. Manly Commando liked that.

I looked out the window and noticed the sun shining, so out I went to the mailbox. Bills, bills, bills. No letter from a murderer. Then my phone started blowing up with *Adman, there's been another murder.*

I should've seen it coming. Maybe the police did. Sure enough, another body was found with a note. This time it was Kink, a drummer who was part of the house band at Joe's Jazz Jam.

Crap.

Everybody thus far murdered is in Joe's house band or plays or sings there regularly. Or, rather, was in the band until they got killed. I called the detectives and asked if they already knew that. They did not and asked who else was in the band.

On that gig? That's about it, I told them. But Joe had several permutations of the band. The detectives didn't understand, so I explained to them how it worked.

You see, a jam is where players and singers needing stage experience-slash-practice with a band can show up and get that practice. Or established *artistes* want some face time with another audience, so it's marketing for them. Sure, sometimes at a jam you'll get singers and players who think they're all that but aren't. But that's not often. Except for the house band, players and singers rotate in and out at will, but all depend upon the largesse of the bandleader calling them up because if he doesn't call, you don't go. None of those get paid for stage time.

The house band usually consists of the same folks. Now at a jam the house band most always consists of the bandleader, usually he's the horn, and keys, bass, and drums. But the bandleader also has other paid gigs. For these he can contract or expand the band based upon needs. So let's say, for instance, the gig is at a restaurant as background noise: Contract to horn and keys. And, let's say the gig is that he's the show and tickets are being sold: Expand from four all the way up to anywhere between five to thirty or more, depending. Each of these permutations usually has its own name, branding, feel, setlists, and so forth. Also, the members of each of those band versions are not usually set in stone.

There's a first-tier call list. Then everybody else in descending order.

None of these musicians are employees of the bandleader but are self-employed. So a bandleader uses a jam to find good players who know their shit and who might could fill in if his first choice is not available. In other words, players show up at jams to audition. Although there are some folks who don't do music as a living but are wonderful players and who just show up for a musical chin wag with friends.

Last, but not least, while there is a show at a jam that the audience sees, the undercurrent of auditioning is not always friendly. Look, I told the detectives, there are a lot of moving parts to the business of entertaining and creating. Not everybody works well together, and if somebody comes in with an attitude that their shit doesn't stink and that they should be treated like a genius and that the performance is all about them, well, the band just might not be nice to them — and rightly so.

The upshot of this, and the detectives caught on real fast about it, is that the victim pool could get larger or it could already have reached final body count.

No way of telling.

The detectives thanked me for calling. Later that evening I was telling CC about the call to them — that's right, I can tell everybody her name now, Clarissa Celeste Caruthers, but I call her CC — and she was quick to point out something to me that, of course, only she would know what with working in the legal profession.

"Oh, Jesus! You stupid son of a bitch!" she shouted.

"What? What did I do? And, hey! Is that any way to talk to your soon-to-be husband?"

"Baby, calls like that. Helpful calls. They look like you are inserting yourself into the case."

"I don't understand."

"And that's why I love you, you innocent little son of a bitch." I heard her sigh on the other end. "Look. That's one of the first signs from a serial bad guy who is afraid of getting caught. He calls the popo with helpful information hoping mighty hard that the popo will let slip something about the case."

"Uh-huh. And?"

"To them, you are a suspect. You're getting the letters that can't be traced. Now you're calling with information that ties victims together."

"Uh-huh. What's wrong with that?"

"Nothing. Just don't do it again unless you talk to me first. Okay? I don't want to have to be spending money on attorneys and bail instead of my wedding. Love you." She paused. "By the way, what was the urgent CALL ME text earlier?"

I thought hard. "Don't remember. Must've been important. Oh, well. It'll come back to me."

"G'night, baby. Love you."

We spent a minute making kissy noises on the phone and whispering naughty things before hanging up.

12 A Summit Is Called

Well, okay. I understood what CC was saying about inserting into the case. And she was correct. At the same time, people I knew were being killed. And, if the second letter was accurate in what it implied, then these murders were not his first and would not be his last. Obviously he got away with killing his wife and that success emboldened him to kill again. And now he's killed four more and has not been caught. So either he's stupid and just one lucky sumbitch, or else he's very smart and is a planner.

The spelling mistakes in his letters make the case for stupid, but there are lots of smart people who can't spell worth a shit for various reasons. As for the messy handwriting, nobody writes neat these days because our muscles have not been trained to do so. We text.

We type, swipe. But we don't write by hand anything longer than a signature, so our skills in this are sorely lacking.

More importantly, and why I am inserting myself into this investigation, is this: He knows me. I know him. Ipso facto, he inserted me into his drama with those letters. What did he expect me to do with them? Feel like I was being honored that he shared? I bet he has no clue I turned those over to the police, and you know what? I bet his ego is so huge he's not once thought I would do that.

Holy cow! When he finds out, will he kill me? Let's hope not. But still, all these thoughts, and upcoming marriage to my woman, made me realize that we — and by *we* I mean the Jazz community — needed to see if we could identify him before he killed more of us. Look. You agree with me, I'm sure. If you knew a killer was after you and your friends, wouldn't you do something? Of course you would. You wouldn't wait around like a victim in a *Friday the 13th* sequel.

Therefore, I decided to call a summit. I sent out texts to fifteen close friends in my phone that were in the local Jazz population. No, I did not GROUP TEXT. I sent them one at a time and it took me fifteen minutes. Copying the original message and pasting it into new texts helped move the process along quickly. The message said –

my house. sunday. 2:00 pm. secret meeting. life and death. reply if you are coming.

Punctuation wasn't great, but they got the drift. I set the meeting for two in the afternoon because some of these folks play at churches both Sunday morning and evening and I didn't want to interfere with gigs that paid the bills. Within the hour, seven said they were coming, three had gigs, two were out of town, and three said they would try to make it depending on personal things going on. That was pretty good. All wanted to know what it was about specifically. I replied to each that they would find out when they got here… and to make sure that when they parked on the street they didn't block any driveways.

Okays popped back in reply. Two days from now we were going to try to figure out who the murderer was. But here is where my thinking got even more diabolical…or rather, I was thinking more like a cop or attorney …other than I got two (unless another came Saturday), I was not going to mention anything definitive from the letters. If the murderer happened to be somebody I invited, then I wanted that person to let the cat out of the bag.

Then somebody texted and asked if they could invite others. Hell no, I replied, this is a secret meeting. Reply received: Okay.

To prepare for the Secret Summit, as I was starting to call it, I printed out both letters and studied them. I would look at the use of his language as a musical arrangement. Every song has a rhythm. A pacing. A form. That when all is put together makes that song a thing of and by itself. The form may include timing, tempo, chord progression, genre, and so on and so on.

So, what did his letters tell me about him? Where did he tip his hand and give more clues about his identity than he meant to?

Just as I started to read them, I got a text from CC. CALL ME. So I did.

"Hello?"

"Hey, babe," I said. "Everything okay?"

"Ummm…yes…but…"

"*But* what?"

She hemmed and hawed a bit then said, "What kind of wedding are you wanting?"

"What *kind* of wedding? I don't understand?"

"You know. Big? Small? Private? Preacher? Church? Courthouse?" She paused a beat. "What *kind*?"

"I hadn't thought about any of that. I have no opinion. What do you want to do?"

"Well…see…here's the thing. The firm I work for is so excited about me getting married. They all want to come. And…this will make you laugh…my boss said he is licensed to marry and wants to preside over our wedding."

I laughed.

"And…well…I know you've got relatives and friends and we've got a huge room here at work and plenty of parking and they're gonna spring for the food and everything. Soooo…" I heard a small laugh, then, "Whatcha think?"

"Are you saying we can get married and have a big party and it won't cost us anything except what we spend on clothes?"

"Yes."

"Well, of course I'm good with that. Don't we have to get blood tests and licenses and stuff like that first?"

"No blood test in Georgia anymore. But license, yeah. We can do that one day during the day. We have to go together. So, I've got some dates…oh, and before I forget, they want a band. Can you put one together and they will get paid?"

"Sure. Yeah. A paying gig for some friends. Hell, yeah. Sooo…dates?"

And so she gave me five dates to choose from. One month out, two months out, and nine, ten, and twelve weeks out. I looked at my calendar and picked two months out. We had a date.

"This is going to be such damn fun. I'll tell them the date and we'll get busy on the planning. Oh, and what day do you want to get the license and in what county?"

"DeKalb County. Any day."

"Love you!"

She hung up and I did a little dance of joy around the table when I went for a beer in the fridge. Wow. What a great gift her firm was giving us. I'm sure it would be something way better than what we could've afforded or had the patience to put on.

I popped the beer top and went back to the letters. I attacked the letters the same way I do when learning a new composition or song. Look at the notes. See what the key and timing are. Test out the interplay between them. Don't worry about exactitude quite yet. Just get friendly with it.

So, I sipped and read. Sipped and started over. Sipped and revisited phrases. Sipped and read whole paragraphs three times in a row. Jumped around inside each letter and from letter to letter and back again.

One beer was finished and another was calling my name, so I moseyed over to the fridge and grabbed another and moseyed on back to the table and stared at them from three feet away. Was there a pattern in the way it was put on the page? I didn't see one. But of all things, even from that far away, one word popped out almost like it was waving a flag at me.

Remember.

Remember is one of those words we use all the time and never think a thing about it. Remember to get the milk. Remember to brush your teeth. Casual. Not like it was the thing itself, but was simply an order, part of a reminder.

For some reason, though, this word as used here was ringing a bell in my recent memory and it wasn't used casually. It carried great weight like the bridge in a song.

Remember.

But who said it? I couldn't recall. I got a red Sharpie and wrote the word big on a plain piece of paper. Used a magnet to plunk it on front of the fridge. Maybe that would help. I gathered up the letters and put them on my desk, pulled out Sweet Stella and got busy working on my skill set.

13 The Summit

CC spent Saturday night at my house and I took her out to breakfast at the IHOP on Clairmont Road near Briarcliff. Sure, technically it was breakfast time, but it was suppertime somewhere, right? So the Ultimate Steakburger with scrambled eggs and hashbrowns were my morning meal. CC had the Raspberry Crepes, two eggs over medium, and fruit. Big pot of coffee got us started and we happily waited for our food to arrive.

Which was as good a time as any to begin telling her about The Summit I'd called and, of course, she freaked out. What if you invited the killer? Well then, says I being real smartass, hold your friends close but your enemies closer. Have you always been like this? Well, yeah, says I; changing your mind, are ya? She stared at me like I was somebody she did not know, but I told her everything was going to be fine and she shouldn't worry.

Breakfast came and I spent the rest of it trying to calm her down. I'd never seen her like this and wondered what the heck was going on and then — blammo! — I remembered what CALL ME meant the other day.

"Babe, just remembered what I wanted to talk about the other day when I texted you to *call me*."

She looked up, a bite of crepe paused halfway to her mouth. "What?"

"Well, see, now I don't want you to think I'm trying to back out or anything, but I am thinking about how we will live together. I mean, look, other than" — and here I went, sticking my foot in my mouth — "a few guy roommates, I've never shared my house with anybody like we're going to. See?"

She chewed her bite, swallowed, and said, "No, I do not see."

"I'm often out late and after a gig, what with adrenaline running high and my brain going a hundred miles a minute, sometimes I'm up all the rest of the night, you know, cuz I can't sleep and then I sleep during the day."

"And your point is?" She stabbed a piece of bacon into her mouth and ripped off a big chunk.

"My point is, baby, I don't want to deprive you of your beauty sleep."

"You saying I *need* beauty sleep?"

I backtracked as fast as I could on that. "No, no, no-no-no…noooo. Haha. That was a little joke. What I meant to say was —"

She held up a hand and said, "I'm sorry. I know it was a joke. But I'm freaking out too."

"Why? I told you The Summit was going to be fine. I'll be safe."

She rolled her eyes. "Not that, you son of a bitch."

She'd been calling me that a lot lately and I was beginning to wonder if that was her new term of endearment for me. She continued.

"We are going to be living together fulltime. Doesn't that scare you?" I didn't get to answer. "It scares me. I mean, we aren't young, newbie, in *luv* kids. We're older. Set in our ways. Can we change to accommodate the foibles and behaviors and routines and…"

And tears ran down her cheeks. Off came her glasses and she put a napkin up to cover her eyes.

Inside Southern Man knew just what to do. *Go sit next to her and put your arm around her, you stupid sumbitch.* And so I did. *Now whisper sweet somethings in her ear.* And I did. And she started laughing and I gave her a kiss and poured her more coffee and moved my plate next to hers and she put her hand on my thigh and Manly Commando said *HELLO!* I told him it was his turn to pay the bill.

We went back to the house, her smiling and talking and holding my hand, and we did some couple things, wedding planning things, like talk about what color suit I would buy and her dress color and flowers and best man and what do you call the women who stand up next to the bride? Anyway, them things. I said one each for the standup people. We started on the guest list. Then she kissed me, sighed deeply in worry for my safety, and went to her house.

Around two o'clock, guests began trickling in. There was a lot of handshaking and backslapping and catching up at first because some of these guys were so busy they didn't get to see each other very often. But finally, somebody found a bag of chips and dumped them in a bowl and, with beers handed out and happily received, The Summit was called to order.

Misha was the first to pipe up. "Theees iss boot da murrrters, yes?"

That got a reaction from the group. I watched carefully in case one reaction was not in keeping with innocence. I did not see any.

Carl said, "There's been three murders, right?"

"No. Four," David corrected, and ticked them off. "Harley Rose. Sam Lorenzo. J Nick. And Kieran Victor Fritz Fornelli."

"Who?" I said.

"You know — Kink. Kieran Victor Fritz Fornelli is his legal name."

Carl said, "How in the hell do you know that, David?"

"We went to school together and lived next door to each other when we were kids."

They watched while, using my red Sharpie, I wrote those names on a pad of paper and held it up where all could see. "Anybody notice what all these have in common?"

I could see lips moving as names were read over and over, but no light bulbs were going off. Then ding-ding-ding. We had one.

"They are all musicians?" That was Chip.

"No, three musicians and one singer," I said.

Lips started moving again and gears were grinding. Ding-ding-ding.

"I know," said André. "The musicians are all in Joe's house band. The singer sings mostly at Joe's Jazz Jam."

"Yes! And what does that tell us?"

It was painful to watch the gears grind. Patience was something I had to cultivate regularly. Misha finally couldn't take it anymore and put them out of their misery.

"I weel tale," he said. "Somebody ees makeen — how you say…uummm… *tsel'* — targeet on dem."

André's ears were slow, so David translated for him. "Somebody is targeting Joe's band."

André's eyes got big and he said, "I sometimes play with Joe. Am I a target?" He started hyperventilating. Somebody handed him the chip bag to breathe into so he didn't faint. Sucking up salt and tiny chip crumbs into his lungs calmed him down right away. We waited while he coughed it all out.

"That's why I called The Summit today. It's possible. But here's the thing. We know this person."

Carl piped up. "How do you know that?"

Shit. Now I would have to tell them what I got in the mail. Or would I?

Hmmmm…. "Let the Adman tell ya how. Pure deduction." I looked around the room to check reactions again. Everybody seemed genuinely waiting for enlightenment. Everyone except Misha, who was ready to jump in if I didn't hurry it up. "Firstly, we've got ourselves a serial killer on the loose here in our little community. At least, as far as we know, he —"

"How do you know it's a he?"

Misha stared at me like *Well…you gonna tell them about the letters or what?* I ignored him and continued. "Most serial killers are men, soooo…anyway, as far as we know 'he' is not targeting any other Jazz communities, right? Don't we all have ties all over the country? Wouldn't we have heard if murders were happening in New York or Detroit or wherever?"

Everybody nodded like that made sense.

"I've been doing a little reading and it seems that serial killers have a reason for doing what they do. They pick people with something in common —"

Misha interrupted. "Not all de time."

"True. But, I mean, usually they do. And we've got a killer who is killing Jazz people. Jazz. People. That's us. *Us!*" I paused to let that sink in. "I'm sure the police are on it, too, but…these are our friends, people we create with. We've got to put our heads together and figure this thing out."

I nodded my head and sat back in my chair, crossed arms over chest, and waited and…nothing. Then this —

"All I've heard about the murders is just what's been going around. I don't know if they are accurate or not." Heads swiveled to Titus. "I mean, look, we could be making a lot of assumptions based on incorrect information."

Misha stared hard at me again. *Share the damn letters,* his glare said. I ignored him for now with a shoulder roll that said *Hang tight, dude.*

"Okay. That's a good point. Let's go see what the Internet says."

And off we all tramped to my office to look it up. We had a genuine production line going. I printed out duplicate copies of any news articles and official police statements/reports that had any information we could peruse. Titus pulled them off the printer. Misha stapled pages. André passed them around. Somebody grabbed some highlighters and pens and off we tramped back to the table.

Lots of conversation as we read the articles, but what was missing, the one big thing that was missing and that all the guys latched onto quick, was that none of the sources said anything about the Jazz community connection. What the victims did, or had in common, was never mentioned.

"That's bullshit!" Arturo hollered.

Ty said, "Maybe it's one of those *clues* that gets left out on purpose so the killer doesn't know they know." He looked around the table. "Am I right or am I right?"

Arturo's eyes popped open and he said, "Hadn't thought of that. That's sneaky…in a good way."

Misha stared at me. I stared back.

"So, according to these reports, unless the popo are holding something back, we know it has to be somebody familiar with the Jazz community… maybe even a part of it."

"Fuck me!" Gerry yelled.

"Zackly," Misha said and stared at me even harder.

"Adman, why does Misha keep giving you hard looks? Do you know something we don't?"

"Well, Leland, let me think how to answer that." I stared hard at Misha, who stared hard back.

"Tell it to theem," Misha insisted.

I closed my eyes to think.

"Jahhhn, listen me now. You *boyus'*, uh…afraid. You make them *obeshchayu ne govori'* — promise not tell." He looked around at expectant faces and held up a hand like he was swearing in court. "*Obeshchayu ne govori'.* Promise not tell. *Derzhat' v sekrete.* Keep secret. Yes? *Obeshchaniye?* Promise?"

All hands went up. Unless I had lost my ability to read people, it was clear the killer was not in this room. I nodded my head and gave them a stern warning because, after all, it was my life now on the line and I was about to get married. I didn't need a widow that fast.

"Okay. I'll tell you. But you better listen to me, you sumbitches. I swear to you that what you're about to hear, if it gets out into the public, could get around to the killer and he will know from whence this information came."

"Fuck me!" Gerry's favorite expression. "You know who the killer is?"

"No. But I do know something. I'm telling you guys. I'm getting ready to get married and I don't want to be dead at my wedding, *capiche*?" I stared hard at each one. "I mean it. No talking to your girlfriend or mama or best bud. This stays here."

"You told Misha," Carl whined.

"Shut up, Carl," Leland scolded. "Misha is Russian. He knows KGB stuff. He's helpful in these matters."

Misha laughed and the tension was broken. But my point was made and everybody accepted it.

"Okay." I stood. "I'll get the letters."

The group erupted with *Letters?* and a few choice curse words including Gerry's favorite. I got my copies and returned. Then I read them both, out loud to the group. I'm going to guess and say that you'd probably like to read both letters in their entirety, too. So I will include both letters here for you to read along with the guys. I gave one more announcement.

"So, I'm going to read it out loud. If you have a question, stop me and let's talk about it. It could be a clue."

Nods all around and I began.

14 Letters Transcribed

FIRST LETTER:

Four handwritten pages.

Dear Adman,

I want to think you for beng friend. You always ben nice to me and I appreciate that. You have nothing to fear from me. Ever. I mean it. I swear. But some folks in this world don't know the pain they visit upon me regular and don't have to when they could just as easy be frindly and we could all get along but they don't be nice and they don't smile and thy always putting me down and insulting me and saying bad things and it's just not right.

I know you agree with me on this because I've seen how you look at them when they get mean and catty and koi and I seen how you don't like it when they try to drag you in on there putdowns.

That's right. I seen you stand up for the little guy and I know I'm a little guy don't mean much in this world but even little guys got to be treated nice cuz there ain't no cause or reason for it otherwise. But do they learn there lesson? Know *they don't. They miss every nice thing you do and just act like the mean fuckers that they are.*

So I had to do something I tell you I had to do something and I couldn't wait no longer. Lessons had to be taught and maybe somebody would learn from those lessons but not the ones I teach it to because they are dead.

I know you agree that them dying is the best thing I know you do and I want you to know I value your support in my mission. Harley Rose might sing like a songbird, but her heart is cold as ice and mean as a junkyard dog and evil as a double-headed rattler even though the rattler is just doing what comes natural the way God intended. But God did not intend her to be like that. And God didn't intend Sam Lorenzo and J Nick to be mean either. Don't they see music is supposed to heal not tear apart no they don't see that they use it as a weapon to destroy, enslave, trick

They are taking what God gave them their beautiful talent for making music as he intended and they are using it for evil

evil evil evil evil evil evil evil evil evil evil evil evil evil

You are so nice that it is posible that you do not truly understand how anybody can kill. But killing is easy when the killing is of someone who needs kilin. There is man's justice and then there is God's justice. Both are equally binding. God may know something about them that I don't. But what I know is who needs kilin and who don't.

So I tell you this: You don't need killing. I like you. Just you remember that I like you.

Sincerely,

One Day I'll Tell You Who I Am

SECOND LETTER:
Two handwritten pages

Dear Adman,

Saw you post on FB about getting married. Congratulations, man. I'm happy for you. I was married one time, but it didn't last. We were together for six months when she died, I mean, disappeared.

Hey Im sure your marriage will be happier than mine was. I hope to meet you financee one day. Maybe she'll come out to a jam one night and you can introduce us.

If you haven't heard, I've killed again. This time Kink. Normally, I'm cool with drummers even when they stomp all over me when I'm playing because I know how it is with drummers. They got to have big egos to play something that obnoxious, but somebody has to keep the time, right

But this guy. He cornered me one night and demanded to know what the hell I had played earlier because it wasn't anything he'd ever heard of. Well, just before I shot him, I told him what the song was. He was so airgant, even when he knew I was gonna kill him, soo sooo soooo airgant that he said I had swapped keys constantly during the song and wasn't listening to anybody else on the stage and nobody knew what to play and that I had let the audience down.

Me? Let the audience down? I said it was him that did that. He laughed and I shot him in his precious hand. He cursed me and I shot him again. In his chest. He fell and I said final performance you son of a bitch and I shot him in the fucking face.

I apologize for my language, but now you understand. But, don't worry. I like you. You're one of the good ones. Hey, I'd give you a fist bump, but I'm not at your house. But if I was I would.

Sincerely,

One Day I'll Tell You Who I Am

PS: I sure would like to play with you again one day soon, Adman. I herd you tour with Misha went good. Hey, I'll be you guitar and you won't have to pay it will be an honor.

15 Discussion Ensues.

And here came Gerry again with his favorite phrasing but, of all things, it completely fit what we thought privately. But, yeah, food for thought.

"And so," I summed up, "you can see why you better keep this damn private and I ain't joking." Seriously worried for me now, everyone nodded. "So? Ideas? Comments? Questions?"

Leland said, "I remember Kink telling me about a guitar player that showed up one night and was all over the place. He never mentioned a name."

"Them letters sound like something a Guitar would say."

"Geez, Gerry. I'm a Guitar. I wouldn't say that," Carl shot back.

Gerry held up his hands and said, "I rest my case."

Carl snapped back. "Hey, you listen up, you sum—"

"Shut up," Leland hollered. "We know it isn't all Guitars. Focus!"

Arturo said, "Can I see the letters?"

"Sure." I passed them over.

He stared at them and said, "This looks like a printout, or a copy. Where's the originals?"

Carl piped up, "You gave them to the police, didn't you?"

"Yes, I did, Carl. But, Arturo, I took pictures of each page before I handed them over. Soooo…"

Leland said, "If you've got these on your computer, can we all get a copy so we can study them closer and write our thoughts down?"

Sounded good to me. Somebody said we should order pizza and somebody else said he had to leave for his church gig and somebody else said he had a gig at a brewery. I printed out copies for everybody and those who had to leave for gigs left. That left me and Misha, Leland, Chip, and André. We ordered pizza, drank beer, and took turns reading the letters out loud. Pizza came and we took a break to eat.

Chip reached for a slice of pepperoni and said, "We should make a list."

André wrinkled his brow. "Of what?" he said through his cheese slice.

Chip swallowed his bite, washed it down with beer. "We know it's a guitar player, right? And we know this guy knows Adman, right? And we know he's played at Joe's jam, right? And Adman and him are friends on Facebook, right?"

We threw down pizza slices, wiped grease off hands, grabbed beers, and took off for my computer wherein I proceeded to bring up my Friends list. We went through it one by one. Misha had thought to bring paper and pen and as I called out guitar players' names, why, there before us was a shortlist of fifteen. One of them was the murderer. Had to be.

"Jahhnn! You sssheck poas 'bout marry."

Since I understood Misha-talk, and we thought so much alike, I knew exactly what he meant. I went to my timeline and scrolled to where the announcement had been made. We checked to see if there were any Guitars on our list who emojied or commented.

"Ten on our list are also on this post," David said after he and Misha ticked off the names I had called out.

Chip said, "Being on that post doesn't mean anything one way or the other. The murderer may have seen the post but not interacted, soooo..."

We all nodded. But we had a list; back to pizza and beer to discuss it.

Leland said, "We need to take each one. Write down what we know about that person. You know, start building a perp profile and see who fits."

"Pairprofial?" Misha shook his head.

"Perp. Profile," Leland said, enunciating each syllable, then explained. "Perp, meanin' perpetrator. Bad guy. Profile. Outline of personality traits."

Misha nodded. "Oh. Yes, yes-yesss. Got eet. *Dos'ye*. Official file."

André said, "Not official. More… anecdotal…circumstantial opinion."

Chip said, "Amateur sleuths, that's what we are. Like Father Brown."

"Who?" we all said at the same time.

"Miss Marple?"

"Oh, yeah." Everybody but Misha now understood.

"Who are these people?" he asked.

André said, "Fictional characters from English cozy mystery authors.

These have been made into movies and TV series."

We stared at André. He said, "My mother is a cozy author, so I know about that stuff."

"What is a cozy author?" we said altogether as one.

André was happy to tell us. "You see, you got your International thrillers. And you got your hard-boiled mysteries. Both of those have graphic violence and sex front and center. But, there are people who don't like all that graphic stuff, but they like mysteries."

He paused while we cogitated. We nodded our heads and he continued.

"So, cozies have murders and sex, but — and this is key — those may be the reason for the story, but nothing graphic and the story doesn't dwell on those. In fact, often these are joked about in a…you know…a humorous kind of way. Plus, in cozies all the crime and the detection take place in a socially intimate community."

He waited again for us to nod, but we didn't, so he finished. "You know…like a Jazz community?"

We nodded and the Amateur Sleuth Society got busy building our dossiers.

16 The *Somno Interrúpta* of an Amateur Sleuth

Empty pizza boxes and beer cans and chip bags piled higher in the middle of the table and we were having us a good ol' time narrowing down the suspect list.

First we put together a timeline of the murders. There had to be windows of opportunity to commit the crime. We got that from working back from when a body was found and married that to when a victim went off the radar. It was hard to do with Harley Rose because none of us hung out with her and we didn't know her schedule. We didn't know anything about her at all. But the rest were working musicians and we kept track of them because we all shared gigs and such as that.

After we got the windows set, we then took a look at everyone on our list. To confirm personal memories, emails and texts were consulted to establish dates and times any of us were with a particular person.

Amazingly, we were able to eliminate all but three on our list. Those that came off the list came off because for one or more of the murders one of us at the table could account for their whereabouts. Some were out of town during a window. Some were at back-to-back gigs. One was in the hospital to get his appendix removed.

That left three; none of us could imagine any of them killing anybody, though. But isn't that what made the murderer so good at not getting caught thus far: He seemed like a nice guy? And all three of these were nice guys.

We spent another hour talking them through and were no closer to eliminating any of the remaining suspects. So we called it a night after I reminded everybody to keep their damn mouths shut so we didn't give an advantage to the bad guy.

After everybody left, I got a large, black garbage bag for all the pizza boxes and beer cans and chip bags and hauled it out to the rolling trash container. Tomorrow was trash day, so I rolled the big green container down to the end of the driveway for the early morning pickup. When I got back inside, my phone had just stopped ringing. It was CC, so I immediately called her back.

"Well?" she demanded.

"Well…what?"

"How did it go with your sleuthing?"

"Went very well. We've got three viable suspects." I felt pretty proud about that. I heard CC sigh. "It's all going to be fine, baby."

She fussed at me a little bit and gave me legal pointers and I agreed with her right and left and up and down and she felt better. Then we started making lovey-dovey talk and that is none of your business, so I'll just stop right there. We eventually hung up with smoochy kisses and I fell asleep a couple of hours later on the sofa to the noise of the television. When I woke up, it was four in the morning and an old rerun of "Mannix" was on. I liked the oldies station at night. Besides "Mannix", the station also carried "Barnaby Jones", "Cannon", "Vega$", and "Matt Houston". Now those guys knew how to investigate a murder. I stayed awake for awhile picking up investigative pointers until I stumbled off to bed and fell asleep again.

Waking a second time, it wasn't an incoming text that woke me. It was a clear thought that I knew exactly who the murderer was and how I knew it. But as soon as I was fully awake, that thought vanished like fog at midday.

Poof!

Gone.

And I could not get back to sleep.

Damn it all to hell.

17 Killin' it at Joe's Jazz Jam

Two days later, Tuesday, I packed up Sweet Stella and headed to Joe's Jazz Jam. I had still not remembered my twilight sleep aha moment, but figured if it was important it would come back. Tonight was going to be an even better night; murder wasn't going to be on my mind. No sir. Tonight CC was coming with me. So on my way to Joe's, I swung by CC's and picked her up. She was to be officially trotted out for inspection in front of all my friends. I could tell she was nervous and said as much.

"Are you nervous about tonight?"

She nodded. "You know why."

"Yes I do, babe." So I thought I'd make a joke. "Hey, notice how I just practiced saying *I do*?"

Ahhh…there it was…her smile. I've still got my comedy chops. I reached over and held her hand. Thank goodness for automatic transmissions. Thirty minutes later we arrived. The parking lot was full, so I found a spot down the street about a block. I pulled Stella out of the back seat and slung her around my shoulders, then took CC's hand and walked to the restaurant.

Well, when we walked in you could see word go round the room and heads swivel our way. Everybody wanted to get a good look at the woman to whom I would become the old ball and chain. I saw some folks I knew at a large table up near the side of the stage. They had two empty seats. Somebody was waving us over. Couldn't tell who it was because they were in shadow.

I told the hostess thanks, but that we'd found a seat. She could see them waving us over and laughed. She was used to the Jazz people. They were always changing tables and walking around and talking to their friends. Some hung out in the green room, but I didn't like to do that. I was there to see and be seen; it was networking and it was fan marketing, baby.

We walked that way. When I got closer, I could see the waver was Ruby. She was at the table with other folks I knew, Alfred Goldsmith and Dwango Peavy. Though I'd never met the other fellow, by the way he had his arm around her waist as she stood and that he was smiling our way, I had to guess he was Ruby's husband.

"JAH-aahhn!" I reached out to hug her, but Ruby pushed me aside and reached for CC's hand and pulled her close. She got the hug. "She is beautiful, JAH-aahhn. What is your name?"

"Clarissa, but John calls me CC."

"Clarissa! CC! JAH-aahhn? How do you deserve such a woman?" She said woman like *wummin*, pure Southern.

She waved us to the empty seats and we sat. Ruby introduced her husband to us. "This is my husband, Timothy." Then she introduced the rest of the table to CC. I didn't pay attention to that because I was settling Stella between my knees and then heard my name called from the stage. It was Joe.

"Hey, Adman. Who's that babe that walked in with you?"

I hollered, "My fiancé!"

Whoa, that lit the place up. Joe started blowing the *Wedding March* like it was a New Orleans funeral dirge and the band joined right on in. That lasted about one minute and everybody had a good laugh, including my beloved.

"What's her name, Adman?" Joe blew out his spit valve.

I hollered, "CC!"

"Ceeee Ceeee," he said, drawing out the vowels and trying to sound all mysteriously sexy. "Well, hello, Ceeee

Ceeee. Welcome to the jam. You know we didn't know a thing about you. Seeing you, I can understand why Adman's been hidin' you."

CC waved and smiled at Joe who asked, "You want to play tonight, Adman?" I nodded in the affirmative and pointed to Sweet Stella. "Alrighty, then. We'll get you up here after the next song. Right now, let's get Ruby up to sing…whatcha wanna sing, babe?"

"*Crying Puddles*," she said and sidled on up to the stage. "Ladies and gentlemen, this is a song about the perils of modern dating."

Piano started with a simple single-note repetitive bass riff. G – B flat – C – D – C – B flat. Bass jumped in layering the riff and Piano began the fill. Ruby snapped her fingers in the mic. Drums sat there waiting for the best time to join in. Then she began to sing.

There's a song about
making whoopee.
[Snap! Snap! Snap! Snap!]
And all the time you got
for the opportunity
[Snap! Snap! Snap! Snap!]
To get it good,
put your mind in a muddle.
[Snap! Snap! Snap! Snap!]
[Here is where the drums come in.]
But for me it's been so long
I'm Crying Puddles.

So I got proactive in
looking for a *mahhhnnn*.
[Snap! Snap! Snap! Snap!]
Went to all these websites
that ended in dot-com.
[Snap! Snap! Snap! Snap!]
Saw lots of pictures that said
"Hey, look at us!"
[Snap! Snap! Snap! Snap!]

Followed by offers of
excellent service.
Oh, oh-oh-oh, Puddles.
I'm crying.

[Music solos here.]
[Now back to the singing,
I mean, the talking part
that was comedy.]

Hey, do you want to hear what the
men say to me? They say –

Are you feeling
mean, girl?
And I say, "Uh, yeah." They say –

I can make you
scream, girl.
And I say, "Promises, promises."

But the best thing,
I tell you the best thing

the men say…
and ladies, you know
I'm not lying…
They say –

I got something you
ain't never seen, girl!
Oh-oh-oh, Puddles.

Well, there's a song
about making whoopee,
but a lot of damn good,
lot of damn good it's doing me
in finding a man who's
certified and "bone"-a-fied,
with talent specific
keeping me cross-eyed.
Puddles!
I'm-I'm-I'm
Crying Puddles.

Our drinks had arrived while Ruby was singing. We put them down to applaud as everybody laughed and clapped. Ruby came down and sat next to her husband, and Joe called me up. He called for *One Note Samba* and off we went.

Halfway through, Drums was taking his solo and I looked at the audience. As my eyes swept the crowd, I thought I caught a glimpse one of the names on the murderer shortlist. Only had a couple of seconds. Wasn't sure with any positivity but couldn't think about it right then as it was time to step back in.

Three more saxes, one more trumpet, and a flugelhorn joined us on stage. The wall of sound was fabulous. I looked over at CC to see what she thought of it since this was her first jam. I found her looking at me. I winked at her.

That is, I tried, but that is not a skill I've ever perfected and it probably looked like an artsy-fartsy squint.

We finished with Joe holding out a long, long note at the end. He gave us the sign and we hit it at the very end with him. Applause, of course. There's something about horns that audiences love. The band Chicago — originally the Chicago Transit Authority — was a prime example of horn love multiplying fan enjoyment. I rejoined CC at the table and took a big gulp of my usual. CC had ordered food and it showed up just as I left the stage.

That was a first.

This having-a-spouse thing was gonna be alright.

18 There is no Shangri-la

I had taken CC home the night before. Poor thing wasn't used to that much excitement and staying up that late. She was sound asleep by the time I pulled into her driveway. I shook her shoulder, gently of course, unlocked the doors, and walked around to the passenger side. She was awake-ish by that time. Opening the door for her, I gave her my hand and pulled her out of the vehicle. She stood and leaned against my chest, took a deep breath.

"Thanks, babe," she said.

"You're welcome," I said, and we walked to her front door with my arm around her waist. Using my key, I unlocked the front door. We walked inside. I got her out of her clothes — yeah, yeah, yeah, shut up, y'all — and in the bed, all tucked in. She was sound asleep by the time I locked the deadbolt.

On the other hand, I was still wired and didn't feel like going home and bouncing off my walls. I rolled the windows down and went for a drive. There's something about night that appeals to my soul. I'm not alone in this because we *artistes* — creatives in every discipline — find the still darkness of night a time when our vision becomes obvious. When all the emotional baggage we carry opens and reveals its contents and we feel free to examine it without censure. We are alone with thoughts that expand horizons and we blossom in the knowledge of possibility.

For me, there is one thing missing a lot these days — and not just in the music world, either. It is the challenging of one another to grow, think, step out of that comfort zone; it puts a brake on stretching the horizons of the mind. This process is not without pain but our pain is interesting; it speaks to us; we dialogue with it and argue and fight, and then laugh together as only brothers can. It's the agony and the ecstasy; we embrace both.

To others, though, night is fear of solitude. The quiet dark does not comfort. They will not engage in self-examination. Their pain is a reason for claiming victimhood and throwing all blame for their horrible little lives onto anything — everything! — other than themselves. They mourn all effort because, according to them, it's useless to exert, so they save their energy for when spending it will get them what they want. Oh, how they keen for Shangri-La.

In 1933, fifteen years after the Great War was over and six years before it began to be called World War One, James Hilton wrote *Lost Horizon*. It's the story of a utopian lamasery high in the mountains of Tibet where everything one chooses to believe is so. Where there are no disagreements, but if there ever is, then one backs down and cedes to the other with the greater passion.

In other words, the squeaky wheel with the bigger emotion gets the woman even if that woman happens to be someone else's wife. See? It doesn't matter. Nothing matters except peace at all cost. There is no arguing. There is only listening and validating of the other and eating and mating and living as long as possible, even if that life is antiseptic and fruitless.

One character in the book couldn't stand the idea of a life like that even if it was long. So, he left and went back to a more energetic life, even if war was coming. Because he knew in the real world there is no Shangri-La.

Those afraid of the night are always upset, therefore they never find their peace. They are the ones who are stuck in an emotional mud bog of their own making and they want somebody else to fix it.

But those who embrace the night, they live with the enthusiasm of God who is willing to make mistakes. Sure He is; do dinosaurs and the platypuses ring any bells? He's willing to dialogue with, and listen, to others. At the same time, He is willing to explain and even be questioned about and defend His position to any who do not understand.

How God communicates is not how "religions" claim…whoa, I was getting cold. Which made me wonder what was the time. I looked at the clock on the console and found two hours had passed. But where was I? I pulled off at the SR 2/Battlefield Pkwy exit and into a dirt parking area of an ancient, abandoned gas station and looked at the GPS. I was well past Ringgold, coming to the Tennessee state line. It was time to head back to Decatur.

I rolled up the windows and headed back the way I came. I know they say if you go slow to stay into the right lane, but by law big rigs have to keep to one or two of the far right lanes. They've got loads to deliver and time is money, so they don't want to get stuck behind some slowpoke having himself a nice long reverie. Besides, I didn't want to hold up the next shipment of bananas. There were babies waiting for their mashed bananas and far be it from me to deprive the rug rats of their treat.

Therefore, I went against all those speed demons and their "the left lane is mine, all mine" mentality and took up position in a left lane with cruise control set to the sixty five speed limit. Roll on, trucker buddies, roll on, and set myself to listening to the noise of tires on road and continued with the reverie.

And so having roamed from mind castles to Almighty God to a wedding to domestic bliss, I soon found myself remembering what I forgot that morning I woke up in a fog, and putting two and two together to get murderer.

19 Doing the Math

When I got back home the first thing I did was pull out the letters. You see, that thought I had — and forgot upon waking — was that I knew who the killer was…and had proof. It was in the letter. I stared at the line:

I like you. Just you remember that I like you.

When I read the first letter I had a thought that there was something familiar that I'd heard before…and recently; just couldn't…put my finger on it. But now I did. Reginald Antonio Banks is the killer. His stage name was Reign. Of course I had looked him up on Facebook during the summit of the

Amateur Sleuth Society and found out all of that.

Okay, I see your point. My proof is not direct, more circumstantial, but you must admit it's pretty damning. After all, he's the one who, standing next to me at the bar at Joe's Jam said, "I l-l-like you. Just remember that, okay? I l-l-like you."

And he fit all the parameters. I sent Misha a text with "9-1-1. Call when you can."

No reply. That's when I looked at the clock. Damn. He was still asleep and his phone was off. I was fit to be tied. Now that I knew, it was killing me to keep it to myself. But Misha finally called around nine a.m. and woke me up.

"Huhllo?" I mumbled.

Misha said, "You say call."

That woke me up. I almost yelled into the phone. "Misha, the killer is Reign."

"Rain *who*?"

"Reginald Banks. You know him."

"Oh, Reign! *Chert poberi!*" Misha yelled right back at me.

"What?"

"Goht dahm," he translated.

"Oh, yeah…God damn."

"Now what we do?"

"That's a good question. Let's call the police —"

"Oh-no-no. No. No. No. Bad idea."

"But why? I've already given them the letters and —"

Misha was shaking his head. I know this because he made a sigh like he always does when he's shaking his head. He mumbled something in Russian that sounded like In a Gadda Da Vida bump-boy-muck-tack-tack, so I knew it was an insult.

"What did you just call me?"

"I say you dumb as duck."

"Why?"

Another sigh from Misha. "Neevah go police wiss *idea*." He said that like an idea was just the stupidest thing ever.

In my most smartassery way I asked, "Then what do *you* suggest?"

"Hmmm...." Then silence as he thought. "Call Summit."

That wasn't half bad, so I hung up and sent texts to the Amateur Sleuth Society to come over Friday afternoon because I knew who the killer was but that I couldn't mention it publicly via text quite yet.

The next two hours saw a flurry of texts — some begging for the name, some guessing. Friday was two days away, but there was just no getting together earlier than that and since my evidence was so-called, it's not like I had a letter from him saying who his next victim would be.

The rest of the day was spent shedding and paying bills. I skipped the

Wednesday jam at RLC. I texted my woman that I was going to bed early and that I loved her and that she was hot and awesome and I may have mentioned a couple of things I'd like to do to her and I sure hope she appreciated the gentlemanly care with which I had undressed her Tuesday.

I got back a *nighty-night* in response. A few minutes later it was followed by luscious kissy lips emoji. I smiled and slept solid until the next morning.

DOOR

20 Comes a Third Letter

"Well, hell," I said out loud Thursday afternoon on the street just as a kid rode by on his bike. "Oops. Sorry."

But there it was. Lounging in the metal box like it was a sauna. Nary a care in the world. Full of faith it would be delivered accurately and that I would find it. Another letter. Of course it was from Reginald Antonio Banks. I recognized the handwriting by now, didn't I?

Do I open it and read it? Yes. So I went inside and got vinyl gloves on and opened it and read after photographing and sending to CC, of course. I was not happy with the contents. It was a one-pager.

Dear Adman,

Let me congrats you again on your upcoming wedding. Saw you woman Tuesday and rushed right back to the house to write you this letter. While you were onstage playing I swung by your table and said hello to CC. She sure does seem nice. I like her.

So, hey, man, listen I have one more chore to do and then I'll be moving on. This town is too negative for me now. I've got a job offer in Chicago so I'm gonna take it.

I sure have liked knowing you and I'll keep up with you on FB. All the best to you.

Sincerely,

One day I'll tell you who I am

PS: I'm packing up now and should be out by Monday, but you know, I got my to do list to finish.

Holy barbeque sandwich and sour pickle on the side. What the hell? Where's the detectives' cards? Dammit. Oh, there. On the fridge. I called a number and I called it fast.

Detective M Charlene Love answered. "Hello?"

"Detective Love? This is Adman... uuhh...I mean John Dann. The letters from the killer? Remember?"

"Yessir, I remember," she said. "How can I help you today?"

I detected a certain cold wariness in her voice. Maybe CC was right when she said too much insertion in the case made the cops wary. But this was no time to think about me. I blurted out, "Another letter came today. I know you'll want it. I can bring it. But I think I should read it to you first."

"Okay. Read it. Hey, hang on. Imma put you on speakerphone so my partner can hear."

So I waited until she said go and I read. She whistled when I got through and they both said Jesus. Detective Mick said, "Are you home?"

"I am."

"Stay there. We're coming now. About an hour away."

"Okay."

I called CC and told her what was going on. She said she'd come if I needed her, but I told her not to worry. Then I called Misha and read him the letter. I also texted CC and Misha the picture of the letter and emailed them to myself. Sure enough, the detectives arrived in about an hour. I answered the door and ushered them to the table.

Detective Mick Hepcutts said, "You shouldn't have opened the letter. What if there was poison powder in there?"

"I'm not worried about that. I know who it is and he likes me."

They stared at me hard. Detective Love said, "You know who it is? And how do you know who it is?"

So, I went through the whole Amateur Sleuth Society Summit meeting and that we deduced it could be one of three men. But that this letter totally cleared two and left only one name because I saw him Tuesday night and the other two weren't there and my fiancé was there and people were talking to her and I had not put it out on social media and hadn't been tagged in any post that mentioned CC from that night, so it had to be him, and now he's got one more target, so they should go arrest him right now.

I believe I said all of that last part in one breath which, for a horn player, isn't that hard, but they were impressed.

"We got to roll on this, so thank you, and we'll head on out," said Detective Mick. They turned to leave then she turned back, laughing. "I just realized the acronym for your group is A.S.S." Both detectives laughed and I did too, then off they went, one on her phone, one driving.

Since there was a clear and present danger — the threat of imminent intent in the letter was clear — they did whatever legal things they had to do to get their hands on him. I do not claim to have any knowledge of the ins-and-outs of those things and so won't even hazard a guess nor try to explain it.

I went on FB and found his profile picture. I took a close-up picture of the screen and texted it to CC. Then I called her and told her what happened with the police.

"Did you get the picture?"

She was very excited. "Yes! Yes! I remember meeting him."

"Oh, man. I am so sorry, babe. Did you read the letter?"

"I did. I'm leaving work and heading straight over," she said.

"Can you get somebody to walk you to your car? I mean, I know he said —"

"I'll get security to walk me out, okay?"

I relaxed and took a deep breath. "Great. I'll see you in an hour. Love you."

"Love you, too."

While I waited on CC to get home — home! — I called Misha and told him what had just happened. Then I texted the Amateur Sleuth Society members and told them The Summit was off and why. It was a long text and I was excited so some of the words didn't come out perfectly spelled when I dictated it, but the point was made and everybody seemed to understand it.

Within the hour CC arrived. I cannot tell you how happy I was to see her safe and sound and not Reginald's target. He's a sick bastard and if there's two things I know about sick bastards is that they can change their minds on the fly and they lie.

CC spent the night. I woke up around three a.m. with some lyrics running through my head. I sat at the keyboard and plugged in headphones and put them on. Began trying various chord combinations. I am particularly fond of F#m, A, and Bm, so I tried it first as a 12-bar Blues.

Hawk flying through rain and fog.
Bark in the distance, of a dog.
I flesh out character, a demagogue,
write his diabolical dialogue.

Didn't work as the Blues, but I liked the chords and by five I had something worked out and notes on paper. Obviously I had murder on my mind for those lyrics to come out and even though I loved the chord progression, it was dark, too. I took off my headphones, went to the bathroom — yes, I flushed and washed my hands — then crawled in the bed next to CC. She rolled over, put her back into me in classic spooning fashion. Didn't take me long to get back to sleep.

21 "May I pour?"

Like I said, it didn't take me long to get back to sleep. So deep I went under I didn't even feel CC get up. What did wake me, though, was a man's voice in a whisper.

At first I thought it was a dream when it said, "Adman. Wakey, wakey."

But I knew it wasn't a dream when I heard the voice holler.

"Adman!" Then in a normal tone, "Or would you prefer I c-c-call you John? Wake up! Your l-l-lady love wants you to w-w-w-wake up, too."

Oh, yeah. I was awake but all I saw was a broad silhouette in the door. The hall light was on behind them and their faces were in shadow. But I'd already made one accurate assumption: The man was Reginald and he had CC.

I am not a hostage negotiator. I've never even played one on TV. But I can tell you one thing. I've always been good during emergencies. Talents and abilities I didn't know I had just pop right on out. I don't have to think about it. Bam! It's there. But I've never had the life of the love of my life weighing in the balance. So a lot of things went through my head in the time it took me to blink eyes wide open.

One: Reginald had no problem with killing.

Two: He likes payback.

Three: He was not happy with me.

Four: I've got to take away his focus from CC.

Five: I better get a damn good poker face — and get it fast. I was still laying under the covers when I had these thoughts and had not moved.

Poker face in place, I looked him straight in the face, or where I thought his face was, and said hello. Then quickly turned eyes just a touch and said, "Good morning, CC."

"Good morning, John," she replied. "Look who I found in the kitchen."

Whew. Good. Her voice was steady. She even sounded friendly, like we had been waiting all along for our guest to show up. She wasn't freaking out… rather, she wasn't letting her freakout show.

"I believe I know who he is, but the light behind has put your faces in shadow. May I turn on the bedside lamp?"

"Yes, you m-m-may," Reginald said.

"Thank you. I'm going to turn slowly to the lamp. May I do it now?"

"Of course, John. But I'm watching. Don't go for a w-w-weapon. Understand?"

"Definitely. Well, here I go."

I pulled the covers off my body. Thank goodness I had on undershorts. Tighty-whiteys if you must know.

Still lying down, I turned and couldn't quite reach the lamp and said, "May I sit up and —"

"Yes, yes, yes. Be quick."

I pushed myself into a sitting position, turned and switched on the lamp. Ah, there they were. "CC, you okay, babe?"

Her back was to Reginald and he couldn't see her face lined with worry and eyes big, though her voice was still steady and calm. "Oh, yeah. I'm good. We're fine," she said.

I nodded and turned my eyes to Reginald. I crossed my legs and put hands on knees and simply looked at him. There he was. Holding the same semi-automatic 9mm at CC's head. The same one he'd used in the other murders…at least, that was his weapon according to the papers.

I said nothing. Somehow I felt that he needed to drive this bus. My job was to get him to drive it where I wanted it to go. I had to let him think he was in control and that everything he did was his idea — or it would've been shortly. So, I simply looked at him, poker face friendly and not threatening, and waited.

Quiet time is a powerful thing. In music, plays, TV shows, and conversations, a pause is a way of saying *What follows is important and I respect that and I eagerly await what is to come.* I could see the gears grinding in Reginald's brain. Which told me he had come up with this little scenario on the fly. I wasn't his next planned victim. Who had he been going to go after and why did he change his mind and come after me? Oh, yeah, it was me and not

CC he was after because I lived alone. It wasn't a secret; everybody knew. He had no bone to pick with CC and I wondered what bone he had to pick with me. CC was merely a fly in his ointment and now he was confused, therefore a bit slow on the uptake.

Obviously he knew how to break-and-enter quietly. All his other targets he'd thought through. Played what-if. Scoped out the best killing ground. But since I had not been a prime target, he didn't know how this was going to play out. He was not expecting two people.

Still, I waited. CC waited. Seemed like forever but was really only about five seconds before he spoke.

"Adman, I'm very unhappy with you. I thought you were my friend. You were one of the few nice guys."

"I'm still your friend, Reginald. I'm still a nice guy. Hell, you're a nice guy. Geez, we've played together at jams and it was a lot of fun. At least, I…I…I thought so." I punctuated that last sentence with a small shrug and a tiny shake of the head as if I was trying hard to understand. Then I shut up.

"Then why did you send the police to my house?"

I shook my head harder now. "You think I sent the popo to your house? Ahhh, man. No way I did that. Why would you think I'd do that?" That last question was punctuated with some sure-nuff sad shoulder slumping and dipping of the head. I even looked down and didn't look at him, like I was the injured party here.

"You didn't send the police?"

"No. But, Reginald, why were the police at your house? Was it some sort of misidentification? You know, like, one of those no-knock warrants but somebody got the house number wrong?" I turned my eyes from him to her and asked, "CC, isn't that what they're called — no-knock warrants?"

"Yes, that's what they're called," she said. Then she said, "Reginald, you may be wondering why John asked me to clarify. It's because I'm a paralegal. I type up these things all day long."

"So, maybe somebody got your house by mistake? Yeah?"

Reginald listened. "It's possible," he agreed. Now he really didn't know what to do. And I waited again. Then he said, "Ah, geez. Damn. I've got myself into a fine pickle here."

"Look, may I make a suggestion?"

He stared at me for a few seconds, then nodded.

"Okay. Obviously you had a very good reason for thinking I sent the police. But I do not know what that reason is. And so, I'm thinking, you know…to figure this all out…maybe we could go in the kitchen. I'll make a pot of coffee. And…uhhh…we'll just talk it out."

I paused again and looked him straight in the eye. My eyes were wide open. I'd sat up straight in the bed and nodded like this is a damn good idea.

He stared at me again. But no agreement was coming. So I got funny.

"Besides, man, I mean, my fiancé is in her jammies and I'm pretty exposed here in my tighty-whiteys. Can she put on a robe and let me slide on my sweats lying right over there and let's go have some coffee and a chat?"

He pushed CC into the room away from him. It was a gentle push. Nothing mean or overtly crazy. She walked slowly toward me.

"Hey babe, can you hand me my sweats, please?"

CC reached for the sweats and tossed them on the bed. Then she reached for her robe hanging on an over-the-door rack and put it on, tying the sash. Didn't take fifteen seconds. We stood facing him. He backed down the hall toward the kitchen, gun still pointed our general way, and motioned with it to move forward toward him. We followed and arrived at the kitchen about fifteen seconds later.

He pointed to a chair then at CC, and she sat. He took a chair next to her, then pointed at the coffee pot and me. So I ground some roasted beans in my antique coffee bean grinder. Hand-powered. Coffee aroma wafted through. Filter in the top. Grounds in the filter. Water in the reservoir. Pot under to catch the coffee. Power button pushed.

"I'm getting cups, spoons, and cream and sweeteners, too. Okay?"

Reginald nodded. "Sure. Yeah."

But I noticed his weapon was not held as diligently as before, though it was still pointed at CC and he had not relaxed his watchfulness. Unintended shots could be just as deadly as any done on purpose, so not something I was willing to jump all over right this minute to try to disarm him. He was a big fellow and seemed in good shape.

We could hear the water heating, gurgling, spraying onto freshly ground coffee beans.

"So," I began in a friendly let's-figure-this-thing-out tone, "why did you think I sent the police?"

He was ready to talk because there was no hesitation now. "Because of the letters."

"What letters?" Yeah, I played dumb.

"What do you mean *what letters?* The letters I sent you."

I looked from him to CC and back, and she looked from him to me and back, and we both acted like we had no clue what he was talking about.

"You never got my letters?"

"Well, Reign, I can double guarantee you that I would remember any letter somebody wrote to me. Wait-wait! Did you send the letters by email?"

"No, man! Through the United States Postal Service. Real stamp. Real handwriting. Real envelope. I wrote *real letters*. None of that email sh-sh-shit."

CC and I looked at each other. I said, "CC, did you see any letters from him?"

CC shook her head no.

And he believed us because our eyes were innocent-wide; besides, he just couldn't imagine either of us nice people lying. "So…so…you don't know what's going on?" Oh, boy.

Now he was truly worried and even more confused.

We did not stop staring at him and shook our heads negatory. Just then we heard the coffee pot spit out the last of the heated water onto the grounds and

CC said, happily like a good hostess should, “Ooo. Coffee’s ready. May I pour?”

He nodded. I passed cream and sweeteners to Reginald. He poured himself some cream and opened up two blue packets of sweetener and dumped them in.

By this time CC had the pot and was pouring him a cup as he stirred. She threw the whole pot of coffee in his face.

He screamed. Dropped his gun on the table. Clawed his face.

CC grabbed the gun. I jumped him. We fell to the floor. CC called 9-1-1 and told them what we needed.

Then she called Detective M Charlene Love and told her to haul ass because the killer was on the floor with second-degree burns to his face.

22 "Ya dumb sumbitch!"

It took about ten minutes for first responders to arrive. CC felt really bad about burning him, but he was pointing a gun at her after all. Still, she got some cloths and wet them down with cold water and put them on his face. She kept changing it out to keep a cold one on it. Reginald kept moaning. When he garbled out *why?* CC let him have it with both barrels blazing, metaphorically speaking of course.

"Why? You ask why, you dumb sumbitch?" Change the cloth. "I'll tell you why. Because you killed people and you pointed a gun at me and my intended, that's why."

She wet another with cold, wrung it out, swapping cloths again. "So, I am not sorry…you hear me? I am not sorry I had to do what I had to do to live. And yes," change cloth, "we got those stupid letters. How stupid could you be to send them, anyway? I swear to God your ego must be bigger than all of outdoors to think we wouldn't call the cops."

Change cloth. Resume denunciation. "That *somehow* we would feel *special* getting a letter from a serial killer. Well, hell no."

This went on until the paramedics arrived. I simply let her have her say. What a force of nature my woman was. Tough and compassionate, too. All rolled up in one. Well, her reputation was set for the rest of her life, that's for sure. Her phone started ringing about nine a.m. Her office wanting to know where she was. She excused herself and took the call in the bedroom.

Paramedics got Reginald stabilized and prepped for transport. The patrol cops were trying to figure out what happened. I kept telling them to wait until Detectives Love and Hepcutts got there, when up come screaming sirens from the detectives' vehicles. They came in through the front door and went straight to Reginald for a good look. Detective Mick said she'd follow them to the hospital. Detective Charlene Love said she'd get the story here and join her later. Sirens blared as Reginald was rushed to Grady Hospital where the creep would get the very best of burn care available...at taxpayer expense.

We had left the mess in the kitchen, so I invited Detective Love to sit on the other end of the sofa from me. Patrol had already secured the weapon; he gave it to Detective Love and she said he could leave, and out patrol went, happy to leave this mess to someone with a higher pay grade.

CC came into the living room just as she was hanging up with her office. I heard her say, "Yes, we are fine. I'll call you after the detectives leave…Oh, I'm fine. Totally fine. I'll probably have a meltdown a little later, but I didn't get hurt, you know, physically… Yeah, he's fine, too…Okay…Okay…Yes…Okay…I have to talk to the detective now… Okay…Bye."

CC looked at me, then the detective, and heaved a big sigh. She came to sit down beside me.

Detective Love took her time letting us get out our story, making her notes, getting pictures of the scene. She had already called the crime scene people who were getting latent fingerprints from where Reginald broke in, and taking the official set of scene photographs. Then she had us write our individual accounts while we were in separate rooms and had us sign and date them. CC took pictures of her statement. I took pictures of my statement. We texted and emailed them to each other. Detective Love collected the papers and said she'd be in touch.

Yeah, she said, we might just have to testify…if it goes to trial.

"I'm glad you're both safe. And I hope we can totally make this case against Reginald Antonio Banks stick."

We nodded. It took the crime scene people about an hour to finish up, then they too were gone. We closed the door and fell into each other's arms. CC started shaking. Response to the adrenaline rush. I walked her down the hall to the bedroom and we got back in the bed, covered up, and I held her until she stopped shaking.

Then she started crying.

Between sobs she said, "I'm not crying — *sob, sob, sob* — 'cause I'm" — *sob, sob, sob* — "scared. I'm mad!" Then she screamed into her pillow and cursed a blue streak. I was impressed. Where had she been hiding all that language and rage?

Then it was my turn to have a meltdown. As I watched her deal with the aftermath, I realized I could have lost her. Tears came to my eyes and damn if I didn't just blubber like a baby. So we lay in the bed crying and saying how much we loved each other and then next thing you know we got naked and…oh, it was good stuff. Almost dying makes you feel things on a higher plateau where the air is thinner and your oxygen-deprived brain is seeing things you didn't know existed.

Yeah, it was that good.

Then we began laughing. And we laughed until we laughed ourselves straight into the shower whereupon even the soap bubbles had us laughing like crazy people. We finally settled down about an hour after midday. Dressed our bodies; made sandwiches, ate them. CC called her office. I called Misha, who said he was coming straight over. I texted the Amateur Sleuth Society with the broad strokes of the event. Several said they were on their way over, too.

Misha arrived first. First thing he did was go to CC and hug her. "Are you okay?" Like a protective daddy he looked her over, turning her this way and that to check for injuries.

"I'm fine, Misha. I'm fine." She hugged him and he hugged her back with a vigor borne of alleviated worry. Then he rushed over to me and threw his arms around me. He was saying a bunch of stuff in a Russo-Engla-Franco mishmash that, even without a translator, I knew meant, "You son of a bitch. Don't worry me like that again!"

"I won't! I promise!"

Wasn't long and more guys showed up. Everybody went to CC first, as they should've done. Then we sat everybody down in the living room — some sat on the floor, some dragged chairs in from the kitchen — and told them the tale and answered their questions.

EPILOGUE

Three weeks after we were targeted by a serial killer, we married. CC's firm threw us one big old party, let me tell you. The band I put together kicked it late into the night with a combination of Jazz standards, Rock and Country covers, and some slow tunes with which everybody could end the night hanging on to their own honey-bunnies and getting romantic. We didn't see that as we had already left for the airport.

As a wedding present, various of my relatives pitched in to pay for two weeks of honeymooning in Ireland, Ye Ol' Emerald Isle. Not that it cost them a lot of money, one of my cousins was a travel agent. But, hey, I wasn't complaining. They were happy to see me settled down. They loved CC, as I knew they would.

We consolidated our two households upon returning, sold both small houses pretty quickly, and very soon after that bought a bigger one with a great room I could use as a recording studio. The house had a workshop behind it.

Two years after the event, Reginald Antonio Banks finally came to trial and his *reign* of terror ended. Hey, like how I worked in his nickname there? Anyway, we were called as witnesses. His defense attorney tried to make out like me and CC had tricked him into coming and deliberately set out to hurt him. He claimed the whole thing was a ménage à trois gone wrong. The jury saw right through that, especially since she had helped with his burn by applying cold compresses. She didn't have to do that. Then there were the letters and the other victims and his dead…umm…missing wife and his fingerprints where they ought not be in my house and the gun he brought whose ballistics matched the other four victims.

The families of all four victims were in the courtroom and when the jury said guilty after each count, there was no applause, there was only crying.

The Wednesday Night Jazz Jam at Red Light Café that used to be run by J Nick before he was murdered, and that I ran that one time, continued on with another bandleader. I simply had too much going on and couldn't do a proper job of it, though I subbed every now and then and, of course, showed up to play occasionally.

Misha and I were playing to sold-out shows all over the Southeast for four tours during the two years leading up to the trial. Word went around about the hostage situation and how CC handled it and, since I was her husband, some of her badass glory sold some tickets as they wanted to see the man…blah, blah, blah. I didn't care. I was happy to live in her shade. Still, we made some good money.

And yes, that house with the great room and workshop was bought on purpose. Misha designed the interior of the van so that we could sleep in it and save even more money on motels and hotels. He and I worked on it at a feverish pace. He had the plan. I was the brute force and before we went on the first post-event tour, it was ready.

The roof was cut and raised to give us more headroom. Bunks were built in, decent mattresses placed. There was a place for everything and everything in its place. CC loved it and she gave us two big thumbs up.

I was working on a new album of my original music and featuring collaborations from Misha and Ruby and Alfred Goldsmith and some vocals from Ruby.

Life was good.

~~ THE END ~~

CAST OF CHARACTERS NAMED AFTER REAL PEOPLE:

Misha Stefanuk [stefanuk.com]

Reginald Antonio Banks, "Reign"

Ruth Amy Norris (Harley Rose)

Sam Lorenzo

J Nick

Mick

Kieran Victor Fritz Fornelli, Kink

Rodney Wayne Manley

Alfred Goldsmith

M Charlene Love

BOOKS BY Durden Kell
Whitfield, Nebraska
A Benjamin Turner Novel
(2015)

BOOKS BY Angela K. Durden
Eloise Forgets How to Laugh
(2004)

A Mike and His Grandpa Story: Series
Heroes Need Practice, Too!
(2006, hardback)
(2012, paperback)

A Mike and His Grandpa Story:
The Balloon That Would Not Pop!
(2012)

Opportunity Meets Motivation:
Lessons From Four Women Who Built
Passion Into Their Lives and Careers
(2010, out of print)

Men! K.I.S.S. Your Resume and Say Hello to a Better Job
(2013, audio book)

Men! K.I.S.S. Your Resume and Say Hello to a Better Job
(2013)

9 Stupid Things People Do to Mess Up Their Resumes
(2000, out of print)

First Time For Everything (2018)

Do Not Mistake This Smile (2018)

Music Business Survival Manual (2018)

Navigating the New Music Business as a DIY and Indie
(2015)

Conversations in Hyperreality —
and Other Thoughts Umberto Eco and
Dave Barry Never Had
(2019)

Dancing at the Waffle House (2018)

Nagging Women and Clueless Men (2017)

From Blue Room Books
blueroombooks.com | blueroombooks@outlook.com

Jedwin Smith
I AM ISRAEL
Lions and Lambs of the Land
(2018)

Alan Ray White
Rock Around The Block
(2019)

1960's Pop icon Len Barry
Prose and Cons
(Coming late 2020/early 2021)

9 781950 729050

DEATH in E minor 9[mm]
BLUEROOMBOOKS.COM
DECATUR, GEORGIA

Made in the USA
San Bernardino, CA
31 May 2020

72449714R00135